THE TIDE
WENT OUT

IS THE TIDE GOING OUT FOR EVER?

THE TIDE WENT OUT

CHARLES ERIC MAINE

With an Introduction by
MIKE ASHLEY

BRITISH LIBRARY

This edition published 2019 by
The British Library
96 Euston Road
London NW1 2DB

Originally published in 1958 by Hodder & Stoughton, London
Copyright © 1958, Estate of Charles Eric Maine
Introduction copyright © 2019, Mike Ashley

Cataloguing in Publication Data
A catalogue record for this book is available from the British Library

ISBN 978 0 7123 5237 6
e-ISBN 978 0 7123 6488 1

Cover artwork © David A Hardy/www.astroart.org
Cover design by Jason Anscomb

Typeset by Tetragon, London
Printed and bound by CPI Group (UK) Ltd, Croydon CR0 4YY

THE TIDE
WENT OUT

INTRODUCTION

The End of Humanity?

IT PERHAPS SHOULD BE NO SURPRISE THAT DURING THE 1950S a significant number of British science-fiction novels brought the nation and the world under threat of destruction, perhaps total annihilation. Britain had survived the Second World War but was left with its scars not just in the physical destruction from bombs and air raids, but the mental cost, that of the returning soldiers who had lived through the horrors of war, and of the British at home, in constant fear of invasion. Add to this the growing fear of nuclear destruction following the development of the atomic bomb.

It was inevitable that writers would explore the fear and horror of a nuclear holocaust or some other apocalyptic destruction. The best known of the doom merchants of the 1950s were John Wyndham and John Christopher. Wyndham's horrors usually originated from outer space, notably in *The Day of the Triffids* (1951) and *The Kraken Wakes* (1953) whilst Christopher's were closer to home. His best known work, *The Death of Grass* (1956), in which a virus affects all grains and grasses leading to famine and a breakdown in society, still has resonance today, and also set the model for many later apocalyptic novels. During the 1950s and 1960s society is threatened by snow in *White August* (1955) by John Boland, plague in *A Scent of New-Mown Hay* (1958) by John Blackburn, global deluge in *The Drowned World* (1962) by J. G. Ballard and a

Biblical plague of insects in *The Furies* (1966) by Keith Roberts. There are plenty more.

For our own sanity, writers—and readers—wanted to know how these disasters could be averted and how each of us might react to such threats. So the novels were written from the viewpoint of one or two individuals or a family so that the horrors of destruction could, in part, be humanised. Hence was created what Brian W. Aldiss later dubbed the "cosy catastrophe", "cosy" because somehow the main protagonist seems to avoid the worst of the horrors and survive relatively unscathed whilst all around him is carnage, and also because as the novel progresses there is always light at the end of the tunnel, and so we can read the novel in comparative calm.

One author who both followed the mould and broke it was Charles Eric Maine. In *The Tide Went Out*, first published in 1958, we do see the horrors unfold through the eyes of the main protagonist who manages to weave his way through the chaos and even have an extra-marital affair whilst society falls apart around him. But he also shows us the bleak reality of such horror and it isn't cosy at all. Nuclear tests have resulted in a crack in the Earth's crust into which the seas and oceans start to drain. At the outset people refuse to accept it—a view which will sound familiar to many in the light of attitudes towards climate change—but as the reality becomes inevitable authorities find they have to act, and act fast. But how does government protect society in a world where there are no oceans, and so no rain, no crops and no food? The social, human and ecological problems are enormous—too vast to explore in one novel and Maine quite naturally settles on how one human struggles for survival in a disintegrating world. Maine also shows that "fake news" is far from new.

Disaster novels aren't new either—they date back at least to H. G. Wells's *The War of the Worlds* (1898)—and they aren't solely British, but they have a resonance with British society, especially one that had lived through the Second World War and experienced destruction first hand.

Charles Eric Maine (1921–81) had served in the War, having trained as a signals officer in the Royal Air Force and fought in North Africa. Then he was plain David McIlwain, a Liverpudlian who had been amongst the first wave of science-fiction fans in Britain. He had produced his own fanzine, *The Satellite*, in 1938, with his friend John F. Burke, in which his earliest stories appeared. After the War he continued to work in television and radio engineering, before turning to journalism and editorial work on a television trade magazine. That was when he created his alter ego Charles Eric Maine.

Because of his connections with radio when he returned to writing science fiction he wrote them as radio plays. His first, *Spaceways*, about the first manned space flight in order to solve a murder mystery, was broadcast on the old Light Programme on 30 January 1952. It was adapted as a film in 1953 and Maine novelised it for his first book in 1954. The play and novel established a format that would be a feature of Maine's work. It was written as a thriller, with a strong element of mystery, rather than a science-fiction adventure, because Maine felt this broadened the book's appeal. He was almost certainly right as his books proved very popular in the 1950s and 1960s.

Maine wrote three other radio and TV plays which were also filmed and expanded as novels, before becoming a full-time novelist. His works include *Timeliner* (1955), *The Isotope Man* (1957), *High Vacuum* (1957), *Calculated Risk* (1960) and *The Mind of Mr. Soames*

(1961). His final novel, *The Random Factor*, which considers a parallel timeless world impinging upon our own, appeared in 1971, though he continued to revise earlier books over the next decade.

What distinguished Maine's work from many of his contemporaries was that he usually explored problems from a new angle. He did not have an in-depth scientific understanding, but he had enough that he was able to develop a new idea that would be easily understood by his readers and then push it one step further. In many ways he presaged the blockbuster technothrillers of the 1970s and 1980s, but he always kept one foot in the real world—even if that real world is falling apart.

MIKE ASHLEY

I

THE CAR HAD BEEN DIFFICULT TO START THAT MORNING, AND by the time Philip Wade reached Fleet Street he was already a half-hour late. The car park on the bombed site in Fetter Lane was full. Finding a kerbside gap within reasonable distance of the office took another ten minutes, and that made the time ten-fifty.

It was still raining—the same stubborn drizzle falling from an iron grey sky that hadn't changed colour in a week. Office lights glared resentfully from the high windows. He paused briefly at the newspaper kiosk near Ludgate Circus, scanning the paraded papers and magazines for the familiar cover of *Outlook*, but it was absent.

He caught the newsvendor's eye. "Sold out?"

"No, Mr. Wade. Withdrawn—about half an hour ago."

"Any idea why?" asked Wade, surprised.

The newsvendor shrugged.

He hurried on through the rain to the Stenniger Press building. MacLaren joined him in the elevator, having just come from the lavatories in the basement. He was smoking a drooping home-made cigarette and peering apathetically at nothing in particular through his concave glasses. A good man, Mac, in his day. One time sub-editor on a national newspaper, until he swapped responsibility for alcohol.

"Some trouble with *Outlook*?" Wade asked.

MacLaren eyed him curiously. "Haven't you heard? My dear boy, why should I be the one to spoil your day?" He chuckled briefly and got out of the elevator at the second floor. Mac was an odd-job sub in the Stenniger organisation.

Wade went on to the fourth and kicked his way through the double swing door with the glass panels that announced: *Outlook—Editorial Offices*. The girls in the general office watched him with veiled interest as he hurried across the room and through the reception annexe to the newsroom. There was a quietness about the place that he didn't like—a kind of furtive, restless tension. Even the typewriters seemed muffled and neurotic.

He exchanged greetings with Rouse and Barlow at the news desk and entered his own office. Betty was busy on the typewriter, but she stopped as he came in.

"Good morning, Mr. Wade."

"Morning, Betty. What goes on?"

Betty regarded him with honest if adolescent anxiety. "They're withdrawing the entire edition of *Outlook*. Mr. Willis has gone over to the printing works. And Mr. Stenniger wants to see you right away."

"What's it all about?"

Betty shook her head solemnly. "I don't know, Mr. Wade."

"I'll talk to Howard at the works," he said.

She switched the internal phone through to the printer on the direct line. Howard was in the machine room going quietly mad, they said. Could he ring back?

"Never mind. I'll talk to Willis instead."

Pete Willis, as chief sub-editor of *Outlook*, spent a great deal of time at the "factory", as the printing works was familiarly (and accurately) known. He was always on hand to check and pass machine proofs as the weekly edition of the magazine went to press, and it was rumoured that he could spot a six-point literal at five feet. But Wednesday wasn't normally a factory day for him. The latest issue of *Outlook* was printed and should have been on the bookstalls, allowing a quick breathing space before the next issue began to make its peremptory demands.

"Pete," said Wade, "what the hell's all the panic about?"

Pete sounded more than a little peeved. "Last minute surgery, Phil. Stenniger ordered a remake on the eight-page forme. We have to pull out the centre pages of every copy and print a new insert. Howard is having several babies. We shan't hit the bookstalls until Friday."

"But why?"

"All I know, Phil, is that your five-page feature on this Nutcracker business has to come out. I'm pushing in two short articles and half a page of snippets to make up the forme. We may get the machine running around three o'clock if Howard gets his finger out, but the collating and restitching will take time. If you ask me, Stenniger's round the bend. Howard's here now. D'you want to talk to him?"

"No," Wade said firmly, but Howard came on anyway. There was a plaintive tone in his voice which Wade found immensely irritating.

"Wade," said Howard, "this is lousing up the entire schedule on machine number four. We've got six other periodicals to print. And as for collating and stitching—you *know* that's always a bottleneck."

"I'm sorry," said Wade, "but it's your problem, not mine."

"It's a bit bloody thick. You might tell Stenniger that this is going to cost a lot of money. We've got a machine standing idle for a start, and we'll have to run the day shift on overtime. The night shift too."

"Tell him yourself," Wade suggested sourly, hanging up.

He looked at Betty, young auburn-haired and blue-eyed Betty, who tried so hard to feel the problems that arose in an intense personal way, but only achieved a mild vicarious anxiety. Why the hell should she care, anyway? This was the kind of silly game that adult men played at, putting magazines together, prettily and with considerable arty-craftiness, then pulling them apart again. From typewriter to typesetter, galley proof to page proof, imposition, make-ready and the final powerful throb of the printing machine churning out the sheets. A balanced blend of art and taste and skill and experience and craft and engineering working in unison for one purpose—to make money. Only this week there would be a little less money made because Stenniger had seen fit to change the contents of *Outlook* after it had been printed and distributed.

He sat down at his desk thoughtfully, propping his chin in his hands. Surprisingly he found himself without any immediate reaction. There was an interrogative twist in his mind that temporarily swamped all other feeling. What was wrong with the Nutcracker story, anyway? It was a good imaginative illustrated feature based on the extensive Anglo-American series of H-bomb tests that had taken place in the early summer under the code name Operation Nutcracker. It was a crusading article underlining some of the dangers that might conceivably result from the indiscriminate testing of more and more powerful nuclear weapons. A little sensational and lurid, perhaps, but then there *had* in fact been excessive rainfall in most continents ever since the tests (even in the Sahara, according to the French Meteorological Office), and some of the rain *had* been slightly radioactive (this has been confirmed by D.S.I.R. at Slough who had investigated sporadic interference to u.h.f. radio propagation from radioactive clouds), and there *had* been recurrent earth tremors in the Pacific and the Far East (one of the most severe had occurred only a few hours earlier, devastating smaller towns in the Japanese islands), and there *was* evidence that there had been a measurable fall in what might be called sea level at certain points in both hemispheres, coupled with the spontaneous appearance of powerful oceanic currents hitherto unrecorded. The article had simply attempted to add these facts together to present a comprehensible if imaginative whole, and there had certainly been no breach of security. After all, the H-bomb tests were old hat—they had been fully reported in all the newspapers at the time, and in cinema and television newsreels. So why all the panic?

There was only one way to find out.

Walter Stenniger was chairman of the board of Stenniger Press, a self-made man with a soft heart and a shrewd head. His smooth grey hair still retained the ghost of an adolescent wave, and his firm uncompromising face hinted at a faded virility which, according to rumour, was exploited whenever possible on an opportunist basis, despite or perhaps because of the pastel and featureless Mrs. Stenniger. Publishing, so far as he was concerned, was a balance sheet—a perpetual contest between income and costs. He thought in terms of percentages, but he also had a keen eye for the slick headline and the hard-hitting copy. Some thirty years of his life had been spent in Fleet Street, and few doubted that the next thirty would be similarly engaged. He was a rugged man, big and bony, with pale blue eyes and a deep rasping voice that sounded as if it had been etched with nitric acid. His mind was ambidextrous: it revelled in the solidly vulgar joke and appreciated the dissonant complexities of Sibelius. Above all he was a man of action; he thought simply and cleanly, and his decisions were always clear cut, though his motives were often obscure. He fired the refractory employee with the same bland equanimity as he engaged the untried newcomer. Though he was hated and loved at the same time, he was always respected.

The six periodicals comprising the Stenniger publishing group were a curious blend of the superficially incompatible. *Outlook* was the foundation stone that kept the organisation ticking over, the illustrated weekly that carried a respectable quantity of advertising and brought in the revenue to sustain its sister periodicals during their more difficult moments. The other magazines dealt with boxing, aquaria and tropical fish, factory management, amateur photography and furniture retailing, and between them they held their own, profits varying with the seasonal fluctuations of advertising. Stenniger was always on the look out for ailing independent publications in any specialist field that could be bought out as an act of mercy, to be reincarnated in a new and livelier format; it was in this way that he had built up, and was still building up, his small but significant empire.

Wade had expected his boss to be showing symptoms of a caustic temper, but in fact the reverse was true. Stenniger was lounging back in his comfortably upholstered chair, benignly smoking a cigar. The massive oak desk before him was tidier than usual, and on the white blotter was a small box containing a gold bracelet (whether a gift for his wife or daughter, or just part of one of the many mysterious deals that Stenniger had developed a reputation for, Wade didn't know).

Stenniger waved the other man into a chair and pushed a cigarette box across the desk towards him. Wade accepted and lit up.

"A bad business," said Stenniger, quite complacently. "Don't misunderstand me, Wade. I'm not blaming you. You know my policy. The editor is always right."

Wade didn't feel very mollified. "I'd like to know why the entire edition has been pulled back just to take out a perfectly innocent story about H-bombs."

"Home Office order. I never saw the government act so quick. Ever heard of Sir Hubert Piercey?"

"Vaguely."

"He's a kind of unofficial government department. All by himself. Job is to set up other government departments. That's exactly what he's doing."

"But what has that to do with *Outlook*?"

"I'm coming to it. Don't rush me." Stenniger struck a match to relight his cigar. "One of the new departments is concerned with press and broadcasting. A kind of central information bureau."

"Sounds more like a censorship set-up to me," Wade commented acidly.

"In a way. Sir Hubert thinks there may be a need to control the way in which news is presented. An official directive is going out. All papers and magazines will toe the line."

"I don't like the sound of it," said Wade, frowning, "and in any case I'm damned if I can see any objection to the Nutcracker feature. It was purely speculative."

Stenniger beamed and thumped the desk. "That's the word! Speculative! Sir Hubert said the article was too speculative to be in the best public interest."

Wade considered the remark for a few moments, then gave up. "What the devil does he mean by that?" he demanded.

Stenniger shrugged heavily. "I don't know. You don't know. All the same, the article had to be killed, and we killed it. Not more than a couple of thousand copies of *Outlook* were sold to the public."

"I still don't like it. People will notice the change. It will focus attention on the Nutcracker business. The papers will comment on it."

"The papers won't," said Stenniger, smiling. "They'll be gagged. And the few people who've already bought *Outlook* won't buy another one on Friday. There'll be no talk and no comment."

Wade stood up, feeling baffled and frustrated, but aware that there was nothing further to be said or done. Censorship was a new and sinister factor that didn't make sense. There was no crisis of any significance anywhere in the world, except, perhaps, in the Far East where earthquakes were causing considerable devastation and political unrest. There had to be a reason—a strong and possibly urgent reason—for totalitarian action of this kind, but obviously it was a closely guarded secret for the moment.

He remembered his conversation with Howard on the phone and said: "Howard is worried about costs—machines idling, overtime, and so on. He asked me to mention it."

Stenniger waved a hand generously. "Tell him to forget it. The government will pay all the expenses entailed."

Which explained, Wade thought, Stenniger's air of sleek satisfaction. If ever a man came out of a deal of this kind without showing a profit, his name wasn't Stenniger.

"Another thing," Stenniger went on. "Sir Hubert wants to talk to you. I plugged you hard, Wade—told him what a good man you are. All the rest." He winked confidentially. "Wouldn't surprise me if he offered you a key job in this new government department."

Wade couldn't avoid being taken aback and showing it.

"If I were you I'd accept it," Stenniger added.

Wade tried hard to think of something intelligent to say, but his mind seemed temporarily paralysed.

"It's not that I want to get rid of you," said Stenniger, enjoying the other's confusion. "I wouldn't want to run *Outlook* if you weren't in the editorial chair. I'll be frank with you, but for God's sake keep it under your hat. Secret, understand. Top secret." He leaned forward, spreading his fingers slowly on the desk blotter. "The fact is, Wade, I'm pulling out. I'm negotiating the sale of the entire concern, *Outlook* and the rest, to one of the big groups. My guess is there won't be any *Outlook* at all six months from now."

Stenniger sat back in his chair and ground the stub of his cigar into a cut-glass ashtray. "I'm going to Canada, Wade. Always had a hankering. It's a country with a big future—and plenty of snow and ice."

It wasn't until many months later that Wade understood the true significance of Stenniger's last remark.

Although Wade spent a further ten minutes in Stenniger's office, he learned nothing new; on the other hand, he was able to resolve much of his bewilderment. On the surface the facts were disconnected: government censorship of *Outlook* magazine, the setting up of some kind of official press and broadcasting information bureau, Sir Hubert Piercey's apparent interest in Wade himself, and, most astonishing thing of all, Stenniger's arbitrary abandonment of what was, in effect, his life's work for an unpredictable future in Canada. There seemed to be no point of contact anywhere, no logical sequence of cause and effect. Like one of the Pacific earthquakes the entire situation had exploded abruptly, disrupting the established pattern and routine of life.

There obviously had to be an explanation—one simple basic explanation linking the isolated fragments of the picture together, and Stenniger knew about it—Wade was sure of that. Stenniger had contacts and friends in high political and governmental circles. Whatever had instigated the unprecedented act of censorship had also prompted Stenniger to dispose of his publishing business and clear out to Canada.

Wade found himself doubting the reality of what had happened. Back in his own office the interview with Stenniger was already taking on a dreamlike quality. "Sir Hubert will get in touch with you when he is ready," had been Stenniger's final words, and even they, echoing and reechoing in his mind, had taken on a hollow synthetic timbre. He glanced at Betty—she was doing something with a pencil and a card index in a prosaic methodical manner, just as she did every day. The sense of tension that he had experienced earlier in the day had evaporated completely, and even the astonishing surgery job they were doing on *Outlook* at the printing works no longer seemed extraordinary.

He sorted through the mass of proofs on his desk until he found the five pages of the offending article. The headline, bold and interrogative, asked: *Is The Tide Going Out For Ever?* Alongside, spread across three columns, was a large picture of an H-bomb explosion; even on the coarse proof paper the outline of the immense incandescent mushroom possessed a certain latent terror.

He read the article slowly and carefully, assessing the meaning and full significance of each sentence, and when he reached the end he had found no fault with it. Suddenly the need to talk to somebody became imperative. He thumbed switch number four on the desk intercom unit.

"Sye," announced a husky feminine voice.

"Philip here," said Wade. "You busy, Shirley?"

"Yes—unless you want to twist my arm."

He glanced quickly at his wristwatch. It was eleven thirty-five and they'd been open five minutes.

"I'll twist your arm," he agreed.

He picked her up and took her across Fleet Street to the Globe tavern. The proofs of the Nutcracker article were in his pocket.

Shirley Sye was an ex-model and looked it. She walked with poise and her statistics were still sufficiently vital to attract a second glance from the casual male. Her hair was black and sleek, and her eyes hazel. Her complexion in longshot was mellow suntan, but in close-up sallow. She'd been thirty-five for the past seven years.

Shirley was editor of the woman's section of *Outlook*, a job for which she was adequately qualified, physically and mentally. Mainly she supervised the beauty column, the cookery corner, the fashion page, and the other miscellaneous features slanted at the female reader. Her mind, Wade found, was alert and responsive, but sometimes he suspected that his liking for her went a little deeper. She, in return, didn't exactly hate the sight of him.

They sat together at a small round table in a corner of the saloon bar. Wade was drinking Scotch, and Shirley was on gin and Dubonnet. He had spread the proofs out over the table top, and was explaining the gist of the article to her.

"Operation Nutcracker took place on June the seventh. Three hydrogen bombs were exploded in the Kaluiki group of islands in the South Pacific. The first was at an altitude of about five thousand feet. The second—sea level. And the third was the daddy of them all..."

"I know," Shirley murmured, scanning the printed lines on the rough proof paper.

The third and biggest—she read—*was a new and hitherto untested monster weapon of joint Anglo-American design. It was exploded beneath the ocean at a depth of two miles. The fireball, obscured by an immense curtain of steam, rose incredibly from the boiling ocean like some monstrous incandescent phoenix. The pressure wave rocked seismographs throughout the entire world...*

"It was the biggest man-made explosion of all time," Wade said. "The apex of the mushroom reached fifty thousand feet—perhaps more. Radioactive fallout is still taking place here and there—after six months."

Shirley sipped her gin and looked pensive. "One of these days they'll let loose a really big banger that'll split the world in half," she remarked.

"Maybe they've already done it. Ever since Operation Nutcracker there have been incessant earth tremors—sometimes violent earthquakes—in the Pacific area. Tidal waves, too. D'you realise more than thirty-five thousand people have lost their lives?"

"Mm. No wonder the Japanese are worried."

"The Australians, too. And the West Coast Americans. Buildings were damaged in Los Angeles only last week."

Wade pulled the sheets towards him and selected one bearing an outline map of the South Pacific, with groups of islands boldly marked. His finger moved speculatively across the paper.

He said: "Within four hours of the explosion a number of small islands to the south-west of the proving zone disappeared completely. But in the north-east some new islands were born. You can almost draw in a dividing line between the two."

"What was the official explanation?"

"There wasn't one. Just some pseudo-scientific jargon about subsidence and contour reaction. You know what I think?"

Shirley smiled. She invariably knew what Wade thought, but she realised that the question was merely rhetorical.

Wade's fingernail scratched a line between the islands on the map. "Here—between the islands that died and those that were born—the bed of the ocean was fractured by the third H-bomb. Part of the bed moved downwards. The other part moved up."

Shirley nodded. "That would account for the business of the islands coming and going."

"And the immense tidal wave recorded just after the explosion—it was simply displaced water."

"All this is very interesting, Philip," Shirley remarked, "but it doesn't add up to a breach of security. Besides, you're talking a lot and I can't listen when I'm thirsty."

Wade took her empty glass and his own and had them refilled at the bar, ordering doubles in anticipation of Shirley's thirst, which throve on alcohol. His own, too, for that matter, though drink had little effect on him—at the worst he subsided into a sour, caustic mood of aggressive cynicism without ever losing coherence of speech.

He returned to the table to find Shirley reading the proofs. He sat down, saying nothing, allowing her to continue until, presently, she put down the pages with a sigh and reached instinctively towards her glass.

"I see your point, Phil," she said, "but isn't it just a little far fetched? All this business of the earthquakes extending along the line of the fracture, lengthening and widening it…"

"It could be," Wade pointed out solemnly.

"All right, maybe it could. But where you overstep the bounds of possibility is in saying that the Pacific Ocean is pouring into the crack."

"Why?"

She hesitated, glass in hand, forcing herself to think more deeply than was her custom. "Well, we all know that the earth isn't hollow."

"I didn't say it was."

"Cavities, then..."

"Shirley, we know that the centre of this planet is hot—maybe white hot. But it's cooling all the time. And anything that cools must contract. So, the core of the earth is shrinking continually, breaking away from the cold outer crust on which we live. There *must* be cavities deep under the ground—beneath the oceans."

"Perhaps you're right, Phil," Shirley conceded. "But to go further and suggest that the Pacific Ocean is draining away through a crack in the ocean bed..."

"Not only the Pacific, but the Atlantic too. All the oceans and seas that are interconnected."

She smiled, a little patronisingly, Wade thought. "Phil, there's a hell of a lot of water in all the oceans of the world."

"Sure there is, Shirley. But, you know something, the Pacific Ocean at its deepest point is less than point one per cent of the diameter of the earth. Given a few man-sized cavities beneath the earth's crust you could pour every drop of water that exists into them—and there'd still be room for more."

Shirley finished her drink as if she needed it. "My turn," she stated. Wade didn't argue, but allowed her to have the glasses refilled. He knew from past experience that she was enough of a lady not to insist on buying the second drink, but sufficiently independent to accept responsibility for the third as a matter of course. They were doubles, he noted. It was going to be a long afternoon.

"How's Janet and young David?" she asked.

"Fine," said Wade, "but don't change the subject."

"I thought we'd finished with it. No reason for censorship that I can see."

"Nor me," Wade admitted.

"Unless," she added thoughtfully, "someone in government circles took it seriously." She paused, staring soberly at Wade. "Supposing what you wrote in that article happened to be true, Phil? Supposing the oceans *did* disappear in that way—through a fracture in the bed of the Pacific?"

Wade shrugged. "It would be damned inconvenient for ships."

"You're being facetious," said Shirley accusingly. "But even so, if there were no shipping, mightn't it introduce economic difficulties? No imports—no exports. No grain ships, no oil tankers..."

"That's certainly an angle." Wade paused for a few seconds to roll the idea round his mind, but when he had finished it was still the same idea. "I can't imagine any responsible politician getting excited about it, though, and I can't see why this article"—he placed one hand heavily on the proofs—"should be arbitrarily suppressed because of some remote possibility that ships might become obsolete at some unspecified future date."

"How's about a general shortage of water?" Shirley suggested brightly. "Mightn't that create an emergency?" She picked up her glass and eyed it affectionately. "Not that I ever drink the stuff," she added.

Wade shook his head. "We don't drink sea water, anyway—don't even use it, except for swimming in occasionally. All our fresh water comes from inland lakes and rivers—ultimately from rainfall. They wouldn't be affected."

Shirley finished her drink. "In that case the thing is still as big a mystery as ever, and we've been wasting time talking about it."

Wade glanced at his wristwatch. "I'll buy you a lunch," he offered, and Shirley accepted. They went upstairs to the restaurant. The place was filling up now, with press people and advertising men, mostly with guests, exploiting their expense accounts. A steak, Wade thought. Something thick and juicy to neutralise the whisky.

Shirley said from across the table: "This business of water level—is it still falling?"

Wade nodded.

"How much?" she asked.

"Oh, very little. A foot, two feet—not much more."

Shirley laughed. "Then what the hell are we worrying about, Phil? Sling me the menu."

Wade passed the menu to her, feeling instantly reassured. There was something infectious about the way Shirley laughed, about her superficial approach to life, that dispelled depression. After all, as she had said earlier, there was a hell of a lot of water in the world—too much water, in fact. Certainly far too much for anyone to worry about—even Sir Hubert Piercey.

He dismissed the matter from his mind.

11

ONE OF THE FRUSTRATING THINGS OF LIFE IS WAITING FOR a promised event that does not materialise. In the weeks following the publication of the censored edition of *Outlook* Wade found himself caught up in the same old routine of writing, editing and publishing—a routine which formerly he had accepted with a certain unexpressed pride as the frictionless working of an efficient machine, but which now irritated and unsettled him simply because it was the formula as before. Nothing had changed. Stenniger made no further reference to the sale of his organisation, nor was there any communication from Sir Hubert Piercey. *Outlook* appeared on the bookstalls every Wednesday morning with precise regularity. Winter came—a mild, wet winter—and still the rainfall was more than average, and still radioactive fallout was detected in the most improbable zones of the world.

Wade had kept Stenniger's secret with a certain reluctant determination. So far as everyone in the organisation was concerned it was hot news that would have given rise to speculative gossip for months to come. But Wade said nothing—except to his wife.

Janet was neither impressed nor worried. Indeed, where Stenniger was concerned she invariably adopted an attitude of slightly hostile scepticism. Wade held himself to blame for the discernible bitterness of her response to people and events; there had been an occasion some years ago when he had allowed himself to be swept into an intense if transient affair with another woman. It was past history now, and if Janet had never found out, well—life would have gone on unchanged. She had been rational about the thing, that he admitted. Too rational, perhaps. She had condoned the fact of adultery, but in doing so had twisted their marriage into a shape that he thought was sometimes unmanageable. She had condoned, but not forgiven. And the marriage had survived by sheer dogged effort on both sides in the interests of David, who was eight, and as bright a boy as you would expect to see any place any time.

Janet, despite her ignorance on matters of nuclear fission, produced clear-cut solutions to the problems that had been worrying her husband. The falling water level was simplicity itself, she stated. Hadn't there been a tremendous increase in rainfall throughout the world during the past few months? That's where the water had gone—up into the clouds and down to earth again in the form of rain. And as for censorship, in her opinion the government was perfectly justified. After all, earthquakes were still taking place in the Far East, and thousands of people were losing their lives. There were political issues involved. If it were admitted that the H-bomb tests were directly responsible for the subsequent earthquakes, who could say what complex and even dangerous international situation might not result, with Soviet Russia backing Far East demands for compensation and perhaps forcing a resolution against Britain and the U.S.A. through the United Nations?

Wade had to admit that she could be right.

"And as for Stenniger," Janet went on, "it doesn't surprise me that he's going to sell out. That's his business—buying and selling. Why do you suppose he built up his publishing organisation on salvaged magazines that had practically folded? He got them for a song and made them pay so that he could sell out at the right price at the right time."

Wade sighed and held on to his patience. "You're not being fair to Stenniger, Janet," he protested. "He's a shrewd character, I admit, but he's genuine in his own way."

Janet laughed sardonically. "If you didn't drink so much you'd be able to see through him. I'll bet he doesn't go within a thousand miles of Canada. Bermuda or Florida, more likely—or even the Riviera."

"That's not true. If he said Canada then that's what he meant. In any case, what does it matter where he goes?"

"It matters a great deal to me," she said decisively. "Seems to me that when the new management takes over you stand a good chance of getting an increase in salary—if you haven't got whisky on your breath when you ask."

Wade ignored the stab. "I may not be around," he said flatly. "According to Stenniger the *Outlook* magazine is finished. Firms often buy out competitive magazines in order to suppress them."

"That's exactly the kind of deal I could imagine Stenniger making."

"At least he's playing it square. This government job may be a bigger thing than editing *Outlook*."

"What government job?" she asked with irony. "You're naïve, Philip. Stenniger was just oiling you."

Wade sighed again. He no longer felt inclined to pursue the conversation, if such it could be called. When Janet was in this kind of mood she was inflexible, and sometimes it seemed as if her antipathy towards Stenniger was a coldly calculated thing, a pose maintained for some unstated and unimaginable purpose. Years ago she had worked for Stenniger; she had known the man well, and he hadn't changed in that time, and whether you had liked him or not at the time he wasn't the kind of man you could loathe in retrospect. But if her malice was a pose, what was the purpose of it? A pose to conceal what? He shrugged mentally: there was nothing to hide.

"He needn't have said a word about the government job," he pointed out.

Janet's smile was razor sharp. "It came naturally. He *had* to mention Sir Hubert Piercey because of the censorship. That opened the way for a little soft soap." A pause while she eyed him critically. "He's got you taped, Philip. He knows how to sell you any time."

"I sometimes wonder whether you hate Stenniger as much as you make out," said Wade in resignation.

"So do I," she answered enigmatically.

Wade moved towards the door. "Have it your own way. For the moment nothing has changed."

"Nothing has changed," she echoed. There was eternity in her voice. "And if you're going out, charge it to expenses. Stenniger can pay for your drinks. I need the money."

"And that's about all you damn well need," Wade said angrily.

He went out.

It wasn't always like that, of course. Most of the time being married to Janet was a placid, peaceful business with a normal level of affection and no trace of bitterness or recrimination in conversation or behaviour. Domestic relationships were largely centred around David, and the pervading atmosphere of the marriage was parental rather than amorous.

Wade was sitting on a stool at the bar of the local, sipping whisky and tracing abstract patterns on the counter with the aid of a puddle of splashed beer. The saloon was quiet and almost empty. At a table a middle-aged couple drank stout with ponderous delicacy, and at the other end of the bar counter a cadaverous man in a bowler hat was reading an evening paper and occasionally lifting a glass of pink gin to his mouth in a conditioned reflex action.

"The breakouts," said Wade quietly, vindictively. The breakouts were the trouble. The occasions when the sutures of the old wound broke open, when the malignant disease of an unforgiven infidelity tortured and strained the union of two people. It would pass—it always did. Tomorrow things would be placid once more, and they might even discuss Stenniger in an intelligent, dispassionate manner. Meanwhile...

He emptied his glass and had it refilled. He was sober, dead sober, and all the whisky had done was to create a zone of numbness somewhere at the back of his brain. Perhaps that was the cause of the trouble, after all—the drink, the regular ration of narcotic to desensitise the mind. Janet was right, though she didn't know why. It was an intuitive assessment of his character. Or what passed for a character, he told himself with irony.

Philip Wade—editor of *Outlook*. So what? How did *Outlook* rate in the scheme of things? Not much. Everyone knew that the Stenniger outfit was run on a shoestring, but Stenniger was a good picker when it came to staff. His key men and women were competent and unambitious types, some of them rejects from the nationals, others good conscientious individuals who thought they'd been given a break and were content to stick in a groove for evermore. And the alcoholics, of course—there were at least four in the Stenniger organisation. Funny thing about alcoholics—they could be brilliant people, imaginative and indefatigable workers—when they were sober. Stenniger got his money's worth outside of licensing hours.

And as for *Outlook*—it was strictly small-time. Coming on nicely, but still having circulation troubles. Publicised circulation one hundred and fifty thousand—that was the figure on the rate card. Print run seventy-five thousand. It was a good job the space buyers at the advertising agencies didn't check with the printer.

Wade was being honest with himself. Deliberately he was looking at himself from an outside viewpoint, Janet's viewpoint, perhaps. He was editor of a small-budget magazine trying desperately to break in on the national picture magazine field. Editorial policy was influenced by advertising considerations and by the need for circulation-boosting gimmicks. News was coloured by speculation and by skilfully applied sensationalism. Take the Nutcracker feature, for instance—alarmist stuff, building up a picture of potential world catastrophe on the basis of a few disconnected facts, not wholly confirmed. That was what Stenniger wanted—demanded. And the final payoff was in the number of pages of advertising carried in each issue of *Outlook*. Stenniger would go through each issue slowly and carefully, first counting the ads and estimating the overall revenue after agency commission had been deducted, then he would go through it a second time, weighing up the editorial, looking for punch lines, seeking controversy, and smiling broadly whenever he found something that brushed without touching the law of libel.

Funny how your standards change in twelve years, Wade thought. As a reporter on a local paper in North London he'd been full of the integrity of true journalism, obsessed with the ideal of objective reporting. But somehow the writers with the gimmicks, who found the unusual angles or sometimes manufactured them, always seemed to get the bylines and the promotion. Imagination seemed to be more important than observation. After all, what did the public like best—the great swarming newspaper-reading public? A little dirt, a little distortion, something to make them gasp, something to provide a talking point for the day's conversations. A journalist didn't have to write a report—he needed to write a story. And as often as not the story had to be constructed with the same careful attention to plot mechanics as in a second feature movie.

What am I cribbing about, anyway? he asked himself. I used the same technique. That was how I broke into the pages of *Outlook* as a free-lance, and that was how I came to have a job on the staff a year later, and that was how I came to meet Janet when she was Stenniger's secretary. Fate weaves that kind of pattern. And in the course of time I came to be editor when old Waterhouse retired. He was a has-been, too—a Stenniger special choice, with ex-national newspaper experience, and enough ability to get *Outlook* on its feet after the take-over—until sheer senile decay forced him to retire. A great job I did—I put nearly twenty-thousand on to the circulation figure and in all that time my salary went up by five per cent and somehow I never got round to taking a straight line with Stenniger. Maybe Stenniger isn't the type of man you can take a straight line with—unless you're an attractive woman, like Janet, for instance. She always seemed to get her own way. Stenniger must have had a soft spot for her.

And then came Claire—a phantom from the past. Six short weeks of insanity and sex, and the inevitable showdown with Janet. And the long years waiting for time to heal the wound, watching young David grow from infant to child to boy, slowly, developing his own immature independence. And the bottle... don't forget the bottle. It's your terms of reference, brother, whether you like it or not. It's the fuel that keeps you going, like an automaton, taking life as it comes without reacting overmuch, and the poison that makes you weak and spineless, again taking life as it comes without reacting overmuch.

Wade ordered another drink. There was time for one more—time for two if he made it snappy. But somehow he didn't seem to care. Nothing mattered. Stenniger was a crook, and the government job was a sop, *Outlook* was sentenced to death, Janet was cold and remote behind some invisible and impenetrable barrier, and life was a still, stagnant tide ebbing from nowhere to eternity. *Is The Tide Going Out For Ever?* he asked himself sardonically, recalling the banned article that had, it seemed, triggered off his current problem.

"Who cares?" he said aloud, then finished his drink and left the bar.

Outside in the open air he felt better. The night was dark and wet, and the rain was a curtain of semi-opaque drizzle obscuring the road lights. He walked slowly in the direction of his home, breathing the cold, damp air, allowing his mind to spin idly and retrospectively. He lit a cigarette and inhaled deeply.

You're not trying hard enough, chum, he told himself. You're running away from life instead of facing up to it. You're not being fair to Janet. After all, she stuck by you at a time when you didn't deserve it—and what have you ever done in return? What have you ever done that wasn't done through a haze of alcohol? Or, come to the point, what have you ever done?

As from now, he vowed, things will be different. I'll beat this bogey once and for all. Janet and me will be pals again, like we used to. And I'll put *Outlook* on the map in a big way so that no new management will have the courage to suppress it. There's still time—still plenty of time.

And there was plenty of time. At least three weeks.

The noble resolutions of the night evaporated under the critical influence of daylight and sobriety. They always did. Wade resumed his normal and imperturbable way of life. Stenniger wasn't so bad, and *Outlook* was a good little paper, full of vigour, and as for the drink—it was nothing more than liquid aspirin to help make the wheels go round, and so long as the wheels kept going round nothing else mattered.

Wade, in fact, looked like a man who had no difficulty in keeping wheels revolving. There was something in the shape of him, hard, lean, perhaps a little bony, that suggested controlled power. His face was rugged without being handsome. For a man of forty-minus he had plenty of hair, thick dark hair that sometimes became lank and drooped solemnly over one eye. His movements and mannerisms were relaxed and generally unhurried, and his voice was crisp with implied authority. It was only in his eyes, blue and restless, and perhaps in his habit of stroking his chin pensively, that one could detect a subtle uneasiness, a suggestion that the latent power was static rather than dynamic. It was the power of stubbornness rather than aggression. He applied that stubbornness to the daily routine of work, and the wheels went round, and he was satisfied.

Below the level of day-to-day journalism things were happening, however. There was talk in Fleet Street, rumours that spread from mouth to mouth like a contagious virus, shadows of news stories that could no longer be published because of the embargo. The terms of the directive from the Whitehall office of Sir Hubert Piercey had been precise: all news stories and features pertaining in any way to Operation Nutcracker, or to the Pacific earthquakes, or to sea level statistics, or to government activities in the Arctic, had to receive official scrutiny and approval before publication. Approval was invariably withheld. The significant and worrying thing, so far as Wade was concerned, was that exactly the same kind of press censorship was taking place in Europe and in America—in every country in the world, so far as he knew.

The reference to government activities in the Arctic puzzled him, and, curiously enough, the rumours were mainly centred on that very area. Stacey of the Inter Press agency, for instance, knew for certain that a mammoth development scheme was in progress in the extreme north of Canada, in Grant Land and beyond, and north of Greenland. The Russians, too, it seemed were up to something north of the northernmost fringe of Siberia. And in the southern hemisphere mysterious activities were rumoured in Antarctica. Stacey couldn't say what kind of activities, but according to his source of information, which he wouldn't reveal, immense quantities of materials and engineering plant were being shipped and flown north and south, almost to the poles. Atomic reactors, too, he said.

Other rumours hinted at huge camps of centrally heated prefabricated huts that were being erected at speed on the polar ice caps, and still others implied that vast dumps of food were being established in what was, in effect, earth's natural refrigerator. Wade couldn't make sense of any of this idle talk. In the ordinary way he would probably have dismissed it all as a fantastic over-exaggeration of some perfectly modest Arctic enterprise, perhaps a scientific expedition. What did disturb him, however, was the unmistakable reference to government activity in the Arctic contained in the press directive from Sir Hubert's office.

If the newspapers were debarred from mentioning it, then there was probably considerable substance in the rumours.

Although the news agencies no longer sent in teletypes about fresh earthquakes in the Pacific, it was common knowledge that they were still happening. Cargo boats and tramp steamers returning from the Far East brought lurid stories of new disasters, of rioting in the Japanese islands, and parts of China and Malaya, of martial law and indiscriminate executions.

The water level stories were increasing, too. It was rumoured that in some parts of the world the level of the sea had apparently dropped by anything from four to six feet, and this, it seemed, was causing difficulty to shipping. Many harbours were becoming unapproachable as the water receded. In effect the coastlines of continents all over the world were being extended as sea level dropped.

The same thing was happening in Britain too, although Wade had not yet seen it for himself. It was as if the tide were going out—far, far out—leaving a permanent border of sand and stones and sea bed fringing the coast of the island. In the Mersey and the Clyde and the Thames Estuary, and nearly every other important waterway, dredgers were hard at work night and day in a frantic endeavour to keep the shipping lanes open. Stacey, who seemed to know everything worth knowing, affirmed that the military had been called in to help, and that in some of the bigger estuaries they were using high explosives to clear the silt from the river mouths.

Very little of this rumour and guesswork reached the newspapers, nor was there any official confirmation by radio or television. There was some oblique reference in one or two of the national dailies to a phase of extremely low tides due, it was suggested, to an unfavourable juxtaposition of lunar and solar gravitational drag on the waters of the world. Wade recognised this as pseudoscientific gobbledygook—probably government sponsored. No doubt a great deal of earnest discussion was taking place in Parliament and at Cabinet level, but not a word reached the printed page.

It was all very mysterious and unsettling, and yet life went on from day to day in the same old way. If you ignored the rumours there was no reason to suppose that it would ever be otherwise.

Until the night of the earthquake.

It was a Tuesday night in the second week of January—another of the mild, wet nights that had characterised this freak winter. The time? Wade wasn't sure. Somewhere around 3 a.m. It came to him gradually, in a deep dreamless sleep, that the windows were rattling violently, as if in a gale. Even so he did not fully awaken. The noise was a meaningless phenomenon, unrelated to reality, without significance in the shifting, fugitive dream world in which his mind was meandering.

Then Janet screamed close to his ear. He was alert in an instant and for a brief interval the only sound he could hear was the pounding of his own blood in his head. The windows rattled again, and beyond the windows was a deep-throated rumbling sound, like distant thunder, persistent and menacing. A door slammed remotely. Footsteps were hurrying along the road outside, and he could detect the staccato murmur of excited voices far away.

"Philip!" Janet cried, gripping his arm fiercely. He sat up, struggling to regain mental orientation, and reached for the pendant light switch over the bed.

The room shook. The house shook. Glass shattered and fell from the window into the room. The ceiling caved in with a tremendous tearing crash. Plaster showered down upon the bed in large jagged fragments. Janet screamed again, and from the adjacent bedroom where David slept came the alarmed cry of a small terrified boy.

Wade found the switch and pressed it, but nothing happened. He rolled out of bed, walking over the shards of plaster that littered the carpet and fumbled his way in the darkness to David's room. He held on to the boy, talking to him soothingly and reassuringly as the house continued to shudder, and presently Janet joined him. They stood together, a compact group in the blackness, surrounded by noise, and feeling without understanding the wild thrusting of the floor on which they stood. The excited voices were louder now, and occasionally distant screams punctuated the background noise like sharp erratic needles.

It came to Wade gradually that this was an earthquake. The realisation produced no immediate reaction; it was an impersonal fact, something objective, beyond emotion and feeling. This was what had been happening in the Far East for months past. The ground—the solid, secure ground on which London was built—had broken adrift, was trembling with some supernal ague. The house, so big and hard and rectangular, was rocking and crumbling. It might collapse about them at any moment like a pack of cards. In street after street houses were shaking and people were awake and afraid, perhaps holding on to each other as he and Janet and David were doing, or rushing headlong into the roads in search of safety.

The small bedroom was suddenly illuminated by orange light. Seconds later the dull concussion of an explosion pulsed through the room. Wade crossed to the window and pulled back the curtain. Beyond the rooftops opposite the black sky was stained red—an angry luminescent red.

"Phil," came Janet's voice starkly through the mottled gloom. "Phil—come away from the window."

He moved back, and as he did so the house heaved gigantically for the last time. The window broke with an astringent sound, and glass fell inwards. And then it was over, and the house became still and quiet, and there was only the noise from the streets, the sounds of frightened people and the drone of speeding cars and the swooping jangle of bells as ambulances and fire engines raced into action.

David was trembling and silent. Wade patted his head, and put one arm round Janet's shoulders. Her flesh was cold under the thin nightdress.

"It's finished," Wade said quietly.

"Phil—I'm scared…"

He squeezed her shoulders reassuringly. "Nothing to worry about, darling. Just a slight earth tremor—that's all."

It was a humane lie, he thought. The earthquake had been severe and had probably done incalculable damage. His brain was too numbed and fatigued to attempt to add it up. Something was wrong somewhere. This kind of thing just didn't happen in England. Somewhere behind it in the inexorable chain of cause and effect were the events of the past few months. The Pacific earthquakes, the receding waters, going back to a single point of origin—Operation Nutcracker. The understatement of all time, he thought ironically. Operation Earthbreaker would have been more accurate.

"It's all over," he added quietly and calmly, but he knew he was wrong. It was all about to begin.

III

THE MORNING PAPERS CARRIED NO REFERENCE TO THE earthquake, not because of censorship, Wade realised, but because they had already been printed before the catastrophe happened. Driving into town he saw relatively little sign of devastation, but here and there broken windows, shattered chimney stacks and the occasional wrecked building underlined the events of the night. London looked more like the victim of an air raid than an earthquake.

The explosion and subsequent fire, he learned, had been the result of damage to a local gasometer. Water mains had been fractured in a host of districts, and in some places streets had been transformed into shallow canals through which his car splashed noisily. Electricity and telephone services had been disrupted on a wide scale, but engineers were slowly getting things back to normal.

The office buzzed with excited chatter, as did Fleet Street itself. The early editions of the London evening papers were already on the streets, carrying banner headlines and half-page pictures of the destruction. He bought a copy of each of the papers and studied them in his office. Matter-of-fact stuff, for the most part; factual reporting with no over-emphasis. If anything there was evidence of playing down. That would be Sir Hubert's line—no sensationalism—innocuous journalism treated in the same routine way as unofficial strikes, Underground hold-ups, and minor traffic offences. The banner headlines and the half-page pictures were space fillers—an attempt to make the story look big while writing it small.

In later editions the headlines were smaller and the pictures were across two columns, and by evening the earthquake story had been relegated to the inside pages.

Wade had lunch with Shirley Sye again—it was getting to be a habit.

"Didn't know a thing," Shirley said. "I slept like a log right through it."

Wade harpooned the lamb chop with his fork and amputated a sizeable portion with his knife. He waited until he had consigned it to the mysteries of gastric chemistry before speaking. Shirley was daintily toying with peas.

"Funny thing," said Wade. "There was no feeling of fear. Just a kind of blank tenseness—like in the war during the air raids. You waited and waited—desensitised."

"The general adaptation syndrome," Shirley remarked casually. She caught Wade's eye and smiled. "Sorry. I was regressing."

"That makes sense, too."

"What I meant was—human beings, all living creatures, tend to withdraw into themselves at moments of potential danger. Even the amoeba reverts to a spherical shape to present the minimum of surface area to the enemy."

"We weren't talking about the amoeba."

"Hell, let's change the subject," Shirley said. "Once upon a time I was interested in psychology. Now and then I like to show off. I'm a little crazy. It comes of being a widow."

Wade let it ride for a while. Presently, half a chop later, he said: "You were trying to say something, just the same—weren't you, Shirley?"

She shrugged. "Nothing important. Just this business of the syndrome. In a crisis people behave differently—they revert to some fundamental level. It has to do with survival. Tell me, Phil—during the earthquake did you stop *thinking*?"

He considered briefly. "Maybe I did. So what?"

"So nothing. But that's the way it goes. Given a long-term emergency, people stop thinking for a long time. They act instinctively, emotionally. The intellect tends to become paralysed. Their behaviour is dominated by a survival drive."

Wade finished his meal, making no further comment. Shirley seemed to be trying to prove something that was of importance to no one but herself. But that's the way she was, unpredictable, with quaint byways to her mind that he would never have suspected. General adaptation syndrome, indeed—what on earth had that to do with the earthquake? With anything at all, for that matter?

Over coffee Shirley said: "I've got a feeling Stenniger is up to something."

Wade made no comment. Stenniger's activities were top secret by decree—Stenniger's decree.

"MacLaren saw him getting into a taxi with Holtz of Consolidated Press," Shirley went on. "And Julie on the switchboard told Rouse that Stenniger had made several long calls to Consolidated. You know what I think?"

"I'll buy it."

"He's planning to sell out."

Wade frowned at her, but said nothing.

"It's logical, Phil. Stenniger built up his organisation from nothing. By now it must be worth a small fortune. He's bound to sell out sooner or later."

"Okay," Wade said uneasily. "Supposing he does sell out to Consolidated—all the better for us."

"Maybe—if they retain the staff and don't fold the papers."

"Why should they do that?"

"Competition. The old cartel business. *Outlook* in particular. The other rags don't matter."

"They wouldn't fold *Outlook*," Wade said, conscious of the lie. He felt impelled to elaborate on his statement. "As a matter of fact, Stenniger has already hinted to me that some kind of deal was in the air. But you and I don't have to worry, Shirley. It's a package deal, so far as I know."

"So far as you know," she echoed. "All the same, I think you ought to keep an eye on him, just in case."

"Which eye?" Wade asked. It made Shirley smile and it was a suitable full point to an awkward conversation. Wade paid the bill and they went back to the office.

Wade couldn't have kept an eye on Stenniger even if he had wanted to, for Stenniger did not put in an appearance at the office for three days. In the meantime the earthquake became a curiously unreal memory once the essential services of water, electricity, gas and telephone communication had been restored. The papers had nothing to say on the subject, apart from a minimum of factual reporting in obscure columns. An illustrated feature that Wade had prepared, drawing a parallel between the earthquake and the air raids of the last war, was vetoed by Sir Hubert's Press Bureau. Wade took it philosophically and substituted an article on Moroccan marriage customs which made a little more impression on circulation figures than a hole in the wall.

When Stenniger eventually came back, the first thing he did was to send for Wade. There were two men in Stenniger's office when Wade walked in—Stenniger himself, of course, looking smug and buoyant with a large cigar dangling unlit from his lips, and a small moon-faced man with pale blue eyes and a charming manner. His face was familiar, Wade thought, but he couldn't attach a name to it.

Stenniger performed the introduction blandly. "Philip Wade, editor of *Outlook*. Mr. Holtz of Consolidated Press."

Wade shook hands and said how did you do, and Mr. Holtz murmured something unintelligible and smiled broadly, about half an inch or so. Stenniger waved a hand towards a chair and Wade sat down.

"As from tomorrow morning at nine o'clock Consolidated Press are taking over the entire organisation," Stenniger stated. "Lock, stock and barrel. Papers and personnel."

Wade said nothing. It had been a long time coming, and now here it was—the sell-out, and maybe the pay-off. He eyed his new employer. Holtz was a neat, precise man, correctly dressed in a dark suit with hand-stitched lapels and the corner of an immaculate white handkerchief peeping from his breast pocket. He was a man with an invisible smile concealed behind his lips, but the lips were dead straight, and hardly moved, even when he talked. A man with plenty of money and no vices, by the look of him.

Stenniger went on: "Mr. Holtz wants to meet the executives and key people in the organisation. Starting with you, Wade."

"Naturally," said Holtz silkily, "as editor of *Outlook* you are, in our view, the most important editorial executive. All I wish to say is that there will be no immediate change in policy. I have studied the magazine for some considerable time and am perfectly satisfied." He paused for an instant, rubbing his slender fingers on his lapel as if feeling the quality of the material, then repeated: "Perfectly satisfied."

"Well, thank you, Mr. Holtz," Wade said with a hint of deference.

"That is not to say there won't be changes," Holtz put in quickly. "Small economies in production. Confining two-colour printing to art paper, for instance. And a slight reorientation of editorial slant from a political viewpoint to tie in more closely with Consolidated's own internal policy."

"I see," Wade remarked.

"One more thing, Mr. Wade. The new management require all key personnel to be signed up on a service contract—one year, initially, with the option of renewal for a three-year period, provided"—his lips made the shape of a small smile—"both parties are in agreement."

Wade thought of Sir Hubert Piercey and sucked at his lips thoughtfully. "Well..." he began uncertainly.

Stenniger leaned forward and said: "It's all in your favour, Wade. Something I should have done years ago. Never got round to it somehow. Security for the staff in black and white."

"It is a condition of the overall transaction," Holtz said briskly.

Something stubborn began to harden at the back of Wade's mind. He looked at Stenniger as if he couldn't see him, then at Holtz.

"You mean—no service contract, no deal?" he asked.

"It's rather more subtle than that," Holtz explained. "Naturally in a transaction of this kind we must take steps to ensure that the organisation we have acquired continues to function efficiently and without interruption. We need the security as much as you do. A service contract is a guarantee to both parties in the agreement."

"But it ties me down for a year," Wade protested. "Supposing something came up?" He looked straight at Stenniger. "Supposing I wanted to go to Canada, for instance?"

Stenniger made a quiet grunting sound and stared at the ceiling.

"Is that likely?" Holtz enquired pleasantly.

"Most unlikely," said Wade. What the hell? he thought. Am I trying to prove something? If so I'm doing it the hard way. I'm confused, that's all. Stenniger tells one story about how *Outlook* will fold within six months, and Holtz tells another about how he wants to sign up the staff for a year or more. Where does Sir Hubert Piercey fit into the picture *now* in the labour stakes—if ever he did outside Stenniger's facile imagination?

"All right, Mr. Holtz," he said reluctantly, "I'll sign. If it's a condition of the transaction I suppose I'll have to—we'll all have to."

To his surprise Stenniger looked at him and winked solemnly. That didn't add up, either.

"There's one thing, though," Wade added, "and that's the question of salary…"

Holtz cut him short with a quickly raised hand, as if he were controlling traffic. "All in good time, Mr. Wade. Let us do one thing at a time. I can promise you that all salaries will be reviewed when we have had time to analyse the economics of the organisation as it now exists. At the end of the financial year, perhaps."

Wade did a rapid mental calculation. Stenniger's financial years always ended in July. Add on three months for an audit and that made October. It was a long time to wait.

He said: "I think I'd prefer to have the salary review embodied in the service contract…"

Stenniger did a surprising thing. He stood up with an unlikely burst of energy, said excuse me to Holtz, crossed the room, took Wade's arm, and ushered him out of the office into the corridor. Still holding the other man's arm he turned to face him squarely, and Wade sensed a bleakness in his manner which he had never witnessed before.

"Look here, Wade," Stenniger said quietly and urgently, "what the hell are you trying to do? This deal is virtually signed and sealed. All you have to do is say yes to Holtz and keep on saying it. The others will play ball—damn it, they need the money. Why should you be so blasted independent?"

"But, Mr. Stenniger—"

"Shut up. I'll do the talking. You don't have to sign any service contract. Just stall him, that's all. After tomorrow it won't matter anyway. You'll be Consolidated property and you can do what the hell you like. For God's sake play the game the way he wants it!"

Wade shook off Stenniger's grasping arm impatiently. "Everyone seems to be playing the game the way they want it except me. I'm tired of being pushed around. This is one chance I have to..."

"To what?" Stenniger demanded angrily. "To squeeze a ten per cent increase out of Holtz? You'd squeeze more gin out of a dehydrated grapefruit. I'm doing right by you, Wade, but you're so damn stubborn you can't see it. Listen. *Outlook* won't last more than a few months."

"Why not?"

"Because there won't be any bloody paper left in the country to print on." Stenniger paused, breathing heavily, still irate. "I shouldn't have said that, but you'll find it's true. I've tried to help you, Wade. Sir Hubert Piercey has a job lined up for you. You'll still be alive when the rest are dying like flies. Now go in there and make that little bastard a happy man."

Wade felt as if he had been shot down in flames. It was the Stenniger attack, as it had always been: the aggressive approach, the crisp words, the hint of secret knowledge, and above all the adroit exploitation of the old pals act. He allowed himself to be pushed back into the office.

Stenniger smiled affably at Holtz, who widened his lips fractionally in cold response.

"Sorry about the recess," Stenniger said jovially. "Wade and I understand each other pretty well. Isn't that so, Wade?"

Wade indicated that it undoubtedly was so.

"Naturally he's concerned about matters such as salary. He's due for a review. Overdue. I thought I'd explain things better on a confidential basis. Man to man."

"And did you?" Holtz enquired politely.

"Ask him," said Stenniger, pointing at Wade.

Wade made a tired smile. He felt outmanœuvred to the point of unconditional surrender.

"I guess I was a little premature, Mr. Holtz," he said politely. "Naturally I'll sign a service contract with Consolidated Press. But I'd appreciate it if you'd keep the question of a salary review in mind."

"In a big organisation like Consolidated, that question is always in mind," Holtz pronounced.

Throughout the rest of the day Holtz remained in Stenniger's office, interviewing the editors and advertisement managers of the various magazines. Shirley Sye went through the screening process too, and later that evening, in the Kennedy Club near the Strand, she compared notes with Wade over a glass or two of seventy proof.

"I take it all back, Phil," she said. "Stenniger and Holtz are on the level. I like this service contract biz."

Wade murmured something non-committal.

"What I mean is," she went on, "there's no question of folding *Outlook*, or any of the other 'zines. And there's no question of bringing in Consolidated staff to take over."

"Sure," Wade remarked. "Our jobs are safe enough—for a year at least."

"Longer than that. You and I, Phil—they can't do without us."

"I guess not."

"After all, when you run a paper like ours on a shoestring, the staff become indispensable—key staff like you and me."

"You may be right," Wade conceded without enthusiasm.

Shirley reached across the table and touched his hand. "What's biting you, Phil? Somebody watered your whisky?"

He smiled and took her hand, stroking her slender fingers gently with his thumb. "I've got things on my mind, Shirley. Things I can't even talk about."

"Not even to me."

"Not even to you."

"You make it sound very ominous."

"I don't know. Maybe it is. Or maybe I'm just being taken for a ride."

She smiled and withdrew her hand. "I'd like to take you for a ride, Phil. In a taxi."

"I ought to say that, not you," he pointed out.

"But you never would. I often wonder how you ever came to get married. I'll bet your wife proposed to you."

Wade considered and pretended to think deeply. It was a rhetorical gesture. "I forget," he said. "It was about a hundred years ago."

"I might have had a chance, even then. I wish I'd got to you first. We'd have made a good team."

Wade regarded her steadily. "Shirley, you've been drinking too much. You're getting sentimental."

"You're wrong, Phil. I'm getting amorous."

"Not with me you're not."

He picked up the glasses and strolled over to the bar for refills. When he got back to the table Shirley was retouching her make-up with the aid of a small gilt compact. She looked nice, he thought, in the mellow light of the club. A little more than a chicken and a little less than a hen. Pity about Shirley. Widowhood wasn't for her—she had too much to give of herself, and her personality needed to expand. She was the extrovert forced into introversion by the inconsiderate death of a partner. How had he died, anyway, that Mr. Sye, so many years ago? Wade whirled his mind. Motor crash, pneumonia, senile decay...? Hardly. Then he remembered. Well, cancer was on the cards for anyone. He felt sorry for Mrs. Sye, not Mr., but that's how it was with life.

He sat down facing her and looked at her with a little deeper understanding.

Shirley said: "I've been tapping the grapevine again."

"Where do you keep it?" he asked. "Everyone taps it except me."

"Stenniger is leaving for Canada next week. Taking his whole family."

"Mm. That's quick."

"There's a good-bye party the day after tomorrow."

"Meaning...?"

"Stenniger's hired the room over the Globe. His secretary did all the arranging on the phone. He's laying on a cocktail party for the entire staff."

"First I've heard of it."

Shirley smiled. "You ought to keep your ear to the ground more than you do, Phil. Didn't Howard tell you he was printing invitation cards?"

"Howard never tells me anything. What's the point of cards, anyway? Why can't Stenniger stick something on the notice board?"

"Don't underestimate the man. He likes to do things in style."

Shirley proved to be right. Wade found a gilt edged card on his desk the following morning, printed in a flowing italic script. It was a formal invitation to attend a "Press Reception" (that was Stenniger's little joke) at the Globe tavern the following evening. In the bottom left-hand corner was the tiny word *Cocktails*. Everybody in the organisation received an invitation, right down to Scruffy, the tea-cum-office boy, and half a dozen delegates from the printing works would be there too, Wade learned.

He warned Janet that it might turn out to be a late night. She didn't seem to care overmuch; if anything she seemed slightly sulky, not because her husband might be late, but because the function was in some way unnecessary.

"I do think Stenniger might have included wives in the invitation," she said flatly.

Wade grunted non-committally. "It would have been an idea, but—well, I guess he looks on it as a way of saying thank you and good-bye to his staff, rather than a social free-for-all."

"I suppose I'll see you when I see you," she said.

Wade said nothing, but looked her over in a remote impersonal way. Pretty girl, was Janet. Lithe and shapely, somehow unpoised and natural. Brown hair and brown eyes with plenty of complexion. Plenty of sex appeal too, but a kind of refrigerated sex appeal that didn't thaw too often. What had Janet got that Shirley Sye hadn't? Or vice versa? They were both unique in their own way, but Janet had the advantage of fewer years. On the other hand Shirley had the edge when it came to personality and charm. You could swap them neatly—Janet's body and Shirley's invisible self—and produce something really exciting...

He checked himself abruptly. The trend of thought was wrong

and immoral. A quiet voice whispered sardonically in his mind. *How moral can you get, Philip Wade?* Shirley's a colleague, he told himself, and that's all. Janet's my wife. I made a mistake once, and I never make the same mistake twice.

That night, in bed, in an effort to reassure himself and check the frightening instability that seemed to be undermining his emotions, he embraced his wife tightly and kissed her with a predetermined calculated passion. She responded vaguely. He made the customary overture, but she seemed to withdraw from his caressing hands.

"I'm not in the mood, Phil," she murmured dreamily.

"But, Janet," he whispered urgently, "I need you."

She half turned away from him. "You're taking me for granted," she said.

"What's wrong with being taken for granted once in a while," he said angrily. "Haven't we been married long enough?"

"That's not the point, Phil." She had turned her back to him now and the night had ended before it had begun. "You can't have me just when you want me."

He said nothing, for he knew from experience that there was nothing to be said.

She went on: "I'm tired and you haven't made me feel not tired. You're doing things all wrong. Try again tomorrow." A pause, then: "Oh, I forgot. Tomorrow's the Stenniger party, isn't it? You'll be coming home late and drunk. Better make it the following night."

"I'll think about it," Wade said sullenly. And he did, halfway through the long night.

It looked as if it was going to be a good party. Within the first half-hour gaiety took possession of the assembly, and the large panelled room vibrated with talk and laughter. Stenniger had laid it on very well. There were two bars, one at either end of the room, stacked with a comprehensive variety of bottles and glasses. Everything was on the house, and Stenniger himself circulated round the room with a proprietary air, not drinking, but smoking a cigar and exchanging jovial backchat with whoever he chanced to encounter, whether executive or office junior. Mrs. Stenniger was there too, with her oversweet smile and pale, tired face, striving to be the perfect hostess, but lacking the energy and vitality.

There were some thirty people in the room, more than it had been designed to hold with comfort. The atmosphere became over-warm and, presently, stifling, but in a sense that helped. It created a false sense of confinement, of intimacy, and it made one drink the more, as if the drink would in some mysterious way reduce body temperature.

Wade sought out Shirley, who seemed to be having adhesion trouble with Barlow, of *Outlook* news desk. Barlow went off to get more drinks, at which point Wade took over and shepherded her into the quietest corner he could find. Shirley was already a trifle glistening, in eyes and complexion. She had been drinking quickly and the pervading warmth was having its effect.

"Having a good time?" Wade asked.

She smiled knowingly. "What's the matter, Phil? Jealous of young Barlow?"

"Well, no. All the same, Barlow is quite a character in his own way."

"I think I like it that way."

"Shirley, the night is still young. Better take it easy."

"I've been taking it easy for too many years, Phil. The older I get the more I think that soon enough I'll be taking it easy for evermore."

"Well, well, well..." Wade said in mild reproof. "The life and soul of the party."

Shirley produced a packet of cigarettes and held them out. Wade took two and put one in her mouth. He produced a lighter and they both lit up.

"I just have a feeling about things," Shirley said tonelessly. "I don't know quite how you'd analyse it..."

"I wouldn't," Wade interposed.

"I've been adding two and two together somewhere down in my subconscious mind, and, well..." She shrugged helplessly. "Stenniger wouldn't get out for fun. There must be a good reason."

"Sure. Hard cash."

"More than that. Stenniger was never short of cash."

"Earthquakes?"

"They're only an outward symptom of something else, Phil. Last night I had a dream, and..."

Wade never heard the details of the dream, for Barlow returned at that moment, holding two glasses, and grinning effetely. His blond hair was a little awry, as if someone had ruffled it, and his movements were a trifle unsteady. Wade estimated that Barlow wouldn't remain upright for much longer than you could count on an egg-timer.

Barlow pushed one of the glasses into Shirley's hands, slopping some of the contents on to the grey floor carpet.

"Been looking everywhere for you, Shirley," he said. Then, apparently, he caught sight of Wade for the first time. "I see I've got competition."

Wade exchanged glances with Shirley, then, a little unchivalrously, excused himself and withdrew. From halfway across the crowded room he glanced back and caught a glimpse of Barlow breathing down Shirley's neck (or so it seemed) and holding on to her with one arm. He smiled sardonically. The evening was still young and Barlow would never make it.

He went over to the nearest bar. The bartender was busy at the far end, so he reached out for an opened bottle of Scotch on the counter and helped himself, pouring not more than a quarter of the bottle into a dry glass. He picked up a soda siphon, weighed it speculatively in his hand, then put it down again. He picked up the glass and inspected the amber fluid with a discerning eye. Here, he told himself, is the product of centuries of craftsmanship and experience and know-how, carefully blended, with the precise amount of water content. Who was he to add water or soda and alter its texture, revamp its formula? He drank it neat.

Walking idly across the room he came upon Stenniger in the process of detaching himself from the editor of the photographic magazine, who seemed to be enjoying a new-found eloquence.

"Ah, there you are, Wade," Stenniger said enthusiastically. He turned to the eloquent editor with a murmured excuse me, and conducted Wade to one side of the room.

"I wanted to talk to you," he said quietly, glancing around with a quick bird-like flicker of his eyes. "I know you think I've been leading you up the garden. This business of Sir Hubert and so on. You wait and see."

"I'm waiting," Wade said without feeling.

"One day. Two days. Any time at all. Take it, Wade. Take it."

"Take what?"

Stenniger seemed to sigh impatiently. "Whatever Sir Hubert offers. Take it and hang the lot. In six months' time you'll be glad."

"You seem to know what you're talking about, Mr. Stenniger, but I'm damned if I do. Why should I take it—whatever it might be?"

Stenniger glanced quickly round again, as if doing a radar scan of the room. "I can't go into details. There's a big world crisis coming up. It will pay to be on the right side of the fence."

"Look," said Wade wearily. "Man to man and strictly off the record. What's it all about?"

"You ought to know," Stenniger stated. "You wrote the Nutcracker article."

And that was all that Wade was able to learn from Stenniger, for a moment later his wife joined him, and they talked small talk for what seemed to be an interminable period. And presently more people joined the group, anxious to exchange platitudes with the man who had so recently been their boss. Wade listened for a while, vaguely bored, until he had emptied his glass, then stole away for a refill.

He never quite made it. As he reached the bar he was astonished to see a cluster of glasses tremble of their own volition; a moment later a tall bottle of sherry suddenly fell over on to its side. And then the room was a bedlam of shrieks and noises, and the floor seemed to be shaking violently beneath his feet. He looked around wildly.

The entire human content of the room was moving in a slow but powerful surge towards the door. Overhead the pendant lamp was swinging to and fro in abrupt jagged motions. The floor shook again, and abruptly the lights went out.

Wade cursed furiously for a moment, then pushed his way forward through the darkness towards the corner where he had last seen Shirley. Ahead of him and on all sides, it seemed, was a rolling tide of shouting and screaming humanity. Panic seemed to pluck his mind, but he resisted it in a mood of grim defiance. The floor had stopped shaking and the earthquake was over, but still the people around him fought their frantic way towards the exit.

He did something that surprised himself. He turned around and fumbled his way back to the bar.

In the flickering glow from his cigarette lighter he selected a bottle of Scotch, then, placing the lighter on the bar surface, proceeded to empty as much whisky as possible into the largest glass he could find. He replaced the bottle and was about to raise the glass to his lips when a familiar voice came to him from out of the darkness.

"Pour one for me too, Phil. I need it."

He turned round towards the voice and found Shirley very close to him. It was the most natural thing in the world, he thought. He reached out with his hand, and extinguished the lighter, then, as the darkness swooped upon them, pulled her towards him. They kissed for a long time.

In the course of time someone brought candles, and the stalwarts began to filter back into the deserted room. Wade and Shirley ignored the excited chatter. The earthquake was already something remote, something in another dimension of space. With the return of light, albeit candle-light, they relinquished their embrace and concentrated once more on the serious business of drinking. For Wade it was a matter of priority. The blood was still racing in his arteries and for what he had to do he needed alcohol—enough to make him irresponsible. Enough to make him forget the commitments and responsibilities of the outside world. Enough to give him blind courage to take the opportunity that was his for the taking.

The party was a mere ghost of itself. Some two-thirds of the guests had disappeared, presumably to home and sobriety. Those who had returned were the hardened extroverted types, those for whom an earthquake was an inconvenient and inexcusable hindrance to fun and drink. Looking around, Wade was unable to see Barlow, but then the room was an immense cavern of shadows and it was impossible to discern anybody clearly.

He held on to Shirley's arm, and they waited in the semi-darkness, finishing their drinks and saying nothing to each other. Fragments of conversation reached his ears. *Blasted earthquakes—it's the damn Japs behind it—the whole thing is a Communist trick—not so bad as the last one—the electricity service is a flop—every time there's a tremor the lights go out—I'll bet Stenniger fixed it that way to save money on drinks...*

"Shirley," said Wade quietly, "I'll take you home."

She seemed to shiver against him, and her fingers tightened on his arm. He glanced at his wristwatch. The time was just a little after nine. Janet would be worried, but she wouldn't be expecting him yet, earthquake or no earthquake. She wouldn't be expecting him for a long time. Maybe he could phone her, just to make sure everything was all right, and to justify his absence for the next two or three hours.

He led the way to the exit, seeing only shapes in the candle-light. Shirley followed close behind him. Fleet Street seemed unnaturally deserted, as if pedestrians and cars had sought a long-term shelter, perhaps for the night. More than anything he was conscious of the absence of lights. The black, shining tower of the *Express* building was a gaunt monolith against an ebony sky, and windows stared blackly into the dark cavern of the road. Somewhere remote a telephone was ringing shrilly, unanswered.

He found his car where he had parked it at the rear of Jason's Court. Inside, at the wheel, with Shirley sitting beside him, he could not resist kissing her again. They maintained the embrace for two or three minutes, and Wade knew that the pattern of the evening was already crystallised.

He switched on the engine, and pulled slowly away from the kerb, advancing cautiously into the circle of light cast by the headlamps, driving steadily enough, but conscious of a certain instability in his movements and in his self-control. He turned into Fleet Street and accelerated towards the Strand.

"Where to, Shirley?" he asked.

"Lawrence Avenue—just off Maida Vale."

Silence as far as Aldwych.

Shirley said softly. "It's only a small flat, but comfortable. I make good coffee, Phil. You'd like some coffee, wouldn't you?"

"Sure would," he replied.

She snuggled closer to him.

"I knew it would happen this way tonight, Phil. It had to happen sooner or later, and somehow... well, Stenniger, and the earthquake..."

"All laid on, just for you and me."

"That's right. We can't escape, can we? I mean, we wouldn't want to escape."

"I guess not," Wade agreed.

Driving through a night unrelieved by light was something of a strain, he found. A sobering strain. There was no obvious sign of further earthquake damage, but electricity supplies seemed to have been cut off throughout North London. By the time he reached Maida Vale his earlier mood of calculated abandon had evaporated, and he found himself thinking more and more about his wife and his son. A nagging sense of guilt began to obsess his mind. Supposing they were in danger, perhaps injured? Supposing the house had been damaged, or even destroyed? Or, even if nothing untoward had happened, supposing they were just waiting in the darkness, alarmed and anxious, waiting for him to telephone, waiting for him to come home?

"Just here," said Shirley. "The second block on the left."

He stopped the car outside her door, then looked at the pale outline of her face in the gloom.

"Shirley," he said. "I was wondering..."

"Yes, Phil?"

"Well—maybe I ought to go on home. Maybe something has happened to Janet and David..."

She came closer to him, and touched his cheek. "Forget it, Phil, They're safe. Bound to be." Her lips brushed against his, and the sweet scent of gin hovered ephemerally in the air.

"Come on in," she continued. "I'll make you that coffee I promised."

He stroked her hair gently, but it was a mechanical gesture, as cold as the night.

"An hour ago I'd have said yes, Shirley. Since then I've had time to think. Somehow... tonight isn't the night."

"You're wrong, Phil. Tonight has to be the night. We'd have been at the party until eleven, or later. Phil—what's the time?"

He looked at his watch, couldn't see it, so flicked his lighter. The time was nine-twenty-five. He glanced quickly at Shirley's face, close to his.

"There's time enough," she said.

He put the lighter back in his pocket and turned away from her. Her hand moved softly over his shoulder.

"Don't you want me, Phil?"

"Shirley," he said, "I want you, but I don't want to take advantage of you. It happened this way once before..."

"Once before?" she echoed.

"Oh, years ago. Quite by chance I met a girl I once knew, in another city, in another world. We got together to talk old times and play remember when. We had a few drinks, and somehow…"

"Somehow?"

"Well, these things just happen, of their own accord. We were both married, but she was separated from her husband. I took her home, just like I brought you home tonight."

She seemed to retreat from him in the darkness.

"It all happened so easily, Shirley. We seemed to slip back in time. And so it went on, for weeks. It didn't seem wrong at the time—until I came to my senses."

"She didn't like you to come to your senses," Shirley said with a hint of irony.

"I guess not."

"They never do."

"I made the break. She became angry. Threatening. She wrote a long letter to Janet."

"Which you denied, of course."

"No. I admitted everything."

She laughed—a quick, harsh laugh. "That must have made for domestic harmony."

"I'm still paying the price," he said dully.

She remained silent for a long time, observing him in the darkness. Presently she said quietly: "I can't make sense of you, Phil. You're strong and yet you're weak at the same time. You've got principles, but only up to a point. Deep down you have integrity, but you don't want to have it, because it worries you. You want to be free, yet you prefer to be tied."

"Sure," he admitted, with a certain air of bitterness. "I'm a helluva guy. What is it they say—a crazy mixed up adult?"

"What you need is a real crisis. You're drifting. Living from day to day, hanging on to the routine, afraid to break away. Come a crisis and you'll find yourself."

"Sure—find myself wondering what on earth I should do. But you're right, Shirley. There's something unresolved inside me. I can't figure it, but it's there. I'll be candid. When I offered to bring you home tonight I'd made up my mind I was going to…"

"To seduce me?"

"Something like that."

"What do you suppose I've been waiting for, Phil? Not only tonight. For weeks—months."

He took her hand and pressed it tightly. "I can't do it, Shirley. I get so far. The image is there, and I make the first action to produce the reality—and then it just evaporates."

"Conscience?"

"Not so simple as that. Some inbred standard, perhaps. A kind of criterion of conduct."

"Phil, you're trying to invent fancy reasons, but the truth is you just don't want me. Am I too old—too senile—too sexless?"

He reached out for her in the darkness and held her tight for a few moments. "Don't be silly, Shirley. You're a very desirable woman, and I'm most conscious of it."

"You sound," she said, "like a doctor making a diagnosis."

"You may be right at that."

"But I don't feel like a patient, Phil."

He released her and fumbled in his pocket for cigarettes. He felt for her lips, placing a cigarette gently between them. They lit up together.

A minute or so later she said: "Phil—forget about everything. I'm just being sociable. Let me make you some coffee."

He said nothing.

"I'm a lonely old woman trying to hold on to company for a little while. Don't let me down, Phil."

When he spoke it was with a voice that had already grown distant and dry. "You know that's not true, Shirley. You know what will happen if we are alone together. You want it to happen and so do I."

"Then let's make it happen."

"No," he said decisively.

"All right, Phil. I'm sorry I made myself seem cheap."

He kissed her slowly, cautiously. "That's not true, either."

"Then why?"

"I don't know. Some other day, perhaps. Right now—it's just the wrong place at the wrong time."

She laughed ironically. "There'll never be another day, Phil..." She moved away from him, and he heard the nearside door of the car open.

"Goodnight, Phil," she said.

"Goodnight, Shirley."

The door slammed and she merged into the night. Slowly, pensively, he engaged the gears and let in the clutch. The car moved softly into the darkness.

"Fool," he said to himself, and yet, strangely enough, he felt pleased.

IV

There was another earth tremor during the night, and still another the following morning, but Janet seemed to be taking it stoically enough, and David regarded it as a novelty. Wade stayed home until midday, rigging up a crude battery-operated emergency lighting system. During the morning electricity supplies were restored, but he finished his self-imposed task, went out to the local shopping centre to buy batteries, then tested the circuit. At all events there would be light in the future, come earthquake or come the end of the world.

In the afternoon he went into the office, to find Pete Willis waiting for him with a pile of page proofs from the printing works. The next issue of *Outlook* was already on the presses, awaiting the final okay before the machines started running. Wade settled down to work.

An hour later Willis came in again to collect the corrected proofs.

"Fine," said Wade. "Mainly clean. You can phone the corrections."

Willis took the proofs and flicked through them.

"Good party," he remarked casually.

"Not bad," Wade agreed.

"Trust Stenniger to lay on an earthquake. He always did do things in a spectacular way."

Wade grunted in a non-committal manner.

"You missed all the real fun," Willis went on. "The manager of the Globe gave us an unofficial extension. I was there until one o'clock in the morning, and I wasn't the last to leave."

"Did they carry or throw you out?" Wade asked.

Willis smiled. "I don't remember. Honestly I don't. Stenniger should have come back too. He'd have been delighted. It was a strictly candle-light affair, with the same kind of atmosphere as a pyjama party."

Wade said nothing; he didn't even smile.

"How did you make out?" Willis asked. "Saw you leave early, with that Sye woman. Trust you. Always on to a sure thing."

"Pete," said Wade acidly, "you've got a lurid imagination. I took Mrs. Sye home, that's all. If you think otherwise I'll fire you here and now."

"You couldn't," said Pete, grinning affably. "Not without the approval of Mr. Holtz."

Pete went out, leaving Wade in a disturbed and sour frame of mind.

Wade made no effort to avoid Shirley during the next few days, but strangely enough he didn't see her at all. Once or twice he was prompted to call her on the intercom in the usual way, to indulge in a little harmless backchat, or even to invite her to lunch with him, but somehow he didn't seem to get around to it.

The truth is you shamed the girl, he told himself in a moment of self-criticism. Then a moment later a cynical voice seemed to whisper somewhere deep inside his mind: *She's not a girl, and you couldn't shame her. She offered herself and you declined. You're in the clear, brother. She tried to burn her wings, but got them frozen instead. That's why you haven't seen Shirley since the party. She's suffering from emotional frostbite.*

Cynicism, he thought. He would have to make it up to Shirley sooner or later. For the present—well, there was no hurry. It was kinder to wait for her to make the first move; it might help to restore her shattered dignity.

One afternoon the telephone rang and a strange female voice spoke to him in the earpiece.

"Mr. Philip Wade?"

"Speaking."

"Hold on, sir. There's a call for you."

An interval of some fifteen seconds, then a smooth male voice, pitched low, that purred in remote feline overtones.

"Mr. Wade?"

"Speaking."

"Good afternoon, Mr. Wade. This is Sir Hubert Piercey."

Wade was taken aback for a few moments.

"I was wondering," said Sir Hubert, "if you would care to discuss certain matters with me. Mr. Stenniger suggested that you might be interested."

"Yes, of course," said Wade abruptly.

"Very well. Supposing you call here at my office at your convenience. Ask for Department Five of the International Bureau of Information. At Imperial Court in Whitehall Crescent."

"Yes," said Wade.

"When?"

"Whenever you like, Sir Hubert."

"Today? Are you free?"

"Yes."

"Very well, Mr. Wade. This afternoon, say at three o'clock."

"Yes—I'll be there," Wade said.

He hung up in a faint daze.

Imperial Court, according to the gilt-lettered sign at the main entrance, was the abode of several government departments. They included the Special Investigation Branch of the Inland

Revenue, and an overflow from the Ministry of Agriculture and Fisheries, which occupied the greater part of an adjacent block. The International Bureau of Information appeared to be a recent addition to the list, for the gilt was new and shiny. Wade noted with interest that the Bureau occupied two floors at the top of the building. He ascended in the elevator.

Sir Hubert's office was buffered by two elegant ante-rooms governed by two even more elegant female secretaries. But it was a cold, austere elegance, and their voices were impersonal to the point of disembodiment. If Mr. Wade would care to take a seat they would find out if Sir Hubert was available. An appointment? A condescending smile. An appointment did not necessarily mean that Sir Hubert could be turned on and off like a tap. The appointment was merely an opening gambit. The final act of meeting Sir Hubert could be likened to checkmate in a complex game of chess. They didn't say so, but it was implicit in their tone of voice, Wade thought. However, he got to see Sir Hubert in less than twenty minutes.

Sir Hubert was a small man, a shrunken man, not more than sixty, but with young, restless eyes that moved with quick birdlike motions behind heavy lids. He was bald, and his pink domed head seemed to have been pressed in plastic. His nose was long and inquisitive, but his lips were thin and not brimming with humanitarianism. His clothes were dark and immaculate, with white collar and silver grey tie.

The office was smaller than the reading room of the British Museum, and the carpet wasn't so deep as a snowdrift, but it was of similar colour—an attractive off-white with contemporary shapes scarcely visible in pallid green. The desk in glass and chrome looked like a tesseract, and the telephones were in different colours, like a captive rainbow. The windows were orthodox, and for that reason they looked surprised.

Sir Hubert stood up and leaned across the desk, holding forward a spindly hand with tight shining skin gleaming white over the knuckles. Wade shook the skeletal fingers. Sir Hubert ushered him into a deep, softly upholstered chair, and remained standing, touching the tips of his fingers together with an air of delicacy. There was a hint of ironic humour in his grey eyes.

"I'll try to be brief, Mr. Wade," said Sir Hubert. "I am currently engaged in establishing a new government department which will have considerable ramifications throughout the civilised world. Indeed, one might say that it is merely one department of a new kind of international organisation. My main concern at the present time is to recruit suitable staff, and that, I can assure you, is no easy task."

Sir Hubert blew his nose on a large blue handkerchief. Wade shifted restlessly in his chair and wished that he could smoke.

"My position is made all the more difficult," Sir Hubert continued, "by the fact that I am required to sign on my personnel without explaining the whys or the hows of the situation. In other words, Mr. Wade, I am offering you a job, but I can't tell you anything about it until you have accepted officially and signed the necessary documents."

"I see," Wade murmured, understanding nothing.

"What I *can* tell you is this. The International Bureau of Information is part of a world wide intelligence network—a kind of world brain linking the civilised centres of the world. Through the channels of communication certain vital information passes. This information has to be collected and collated and interpreted. World governments rely absolutely on the information which they receive from us, and from other I.B.I. centres in other countries. We also act as a filter, passing approved information to the news agencies and broadcasting services, or, in some cases, withholding information."

"You want me to become part of this—this filter?" Wade asked.

"Yes, I do," Sir Hubert said crisply. He crossed to the desk and picked up a green folder, referring briefly to the contents. "Naturally we have already checked on you—more than you might imagine. You are an American by birth—educated in New Jersey until you were eleven years old. Your father died, and your mother, who was English, brought you back to London. We've checked on your school records. They are adequate. Your war record as a bomber pilot is even better. We know about your wife and son, and we know about your career in magazine journalism. We know a great deal about your psychological make-up—a tendency towards alcoholism, for instance…"

Wade smiled grimly and without embarrassment.

"Naturally there will be further tests—complete physiological and psychiatric examinations. We are interested in a certain *type* of personality—certain essential requirements of basic psychology. We think you might fill those requirements."

"So what do you want me to do, Sir Hubert?"

"There are two things you must do immediately, and both demand a rather difficult decision." Sir Hubert replaced the folder on his desk and walked around the room with his hands clasped behind his back. "If I had not thought you capable of making these decisions, you would not now be sitting in this office."

"Thank you, sir," Wade felt prompted to say.

Sir Hubert stopped walking around, and turned to face the other man squarely.

He said: "First I need to know whether you are prepared to send your wife and son away for an indefinite period."

"Away...?"

"Out of the country."

Wade frowned, bewildered. "But—where?"

"To a government domestic camp in the Arctic."

Wade stared blankly at the other man for several seconds.

"If you are to work for us then it must be done," Sir Hubert stated firmly.

"But—why?"

"There are very good reasons which will be explained to you in due course. For the moment I require a positive assurance..."

"But how can I give you an assurance?" Wade demanded. "My wife has some say in the matter. If it doesn't make sense to me it certainly won't to her."

"It's up to you to make it seem sensible. You have to convince her that it is necessary—urgently necessary."

"I'm afraid you don't know my wife, Sir Hubert," Wade said sardonically.

Sir Hubert was not amused that Wade could notice. His expression could hardly have been sterner at that moment. He came nearer, pouting his lips, and holding tightly on to the lapels of his coat with spidery fingers.

"Let me put it this way, Mr. Wade. We are on the brink of a world crisis of unimaginable proportions. Governments all over the world are busy recruiting reliable staffs to cope with this crisis. In order to relieve the personnel concerned of all worry and anxiety about their families, steps have been taken to evacuate those families to areas of maximum safety. Believe me, it is in your own interests to do exactly as I say."

"I need time to think about it," Wade said. "What you are asking just doesn't seem reasonable."

"Inside three months it will be only too reasonable. Now for the second point—I want you to decide, here and now, whether you are going to accept the post I am offering."

"But I don't even know what the post is..."

"It will exploit your journalistic ability and your power of imagination."

"But, Sir Hubert—aren't there other details to consider. The sordid matter of salary, for instance..."

Sir Hubert smiled for the first time. "You can have all the money you want, Mr. Wade. In a few weeks it will be worthless, anyway. Well, what's your answer?"

Wade tried to focus his mind, to view the situation in some kind of rational perspective, but it proved to be impossible. And yet he *knew* what it was all about, knew but couldn't define it. Sir Hubert's long thin face was part of a surrealist pattern of H-bombs and earthquakes and falling water levels and mysterious Arctic camps. Get rid of your family, Sir Hubert had said. Send them into the wilderness of ice beyond the Arctic circle. Take an unspecified job with me at a salary that is going to be worthless in a few weeks.

"Well?" Sir Hubert repeated.

"I don't know what to say," Wade murmured uneasily. "If I knew a little more about it..."

"I can tell you nothing more at this stage. But, without saying a word, I *can* show you this."

Sir Hubert returned to his desk and opened a drawer, from which he took a small flat object that resembled a large wallet. He handed it to Wade in silence.

It was a flexible folder, pocket-sized, in black plastic material. Wade opened it slowly. Inside were three printed booklets contained in a pouch. He removed them.

They were of identical shape, and they all contained printed coupons on perforated pages, and at the tops of the pages were headings which announced: *First Period—Second Period*—and so on. The coupons in each of the books were printed on paper of different colours.

On the cover of each book was an official crown, with a title in bold black letters. The first book said: *Food—Basic and Supplementary Coupons*. The second stated: *Fuel—Oil, Petrol, Coal, Coke—Basic Only*.

And on the cover of the third book was one word only—*Water*.

Slowly Wade replaced the booklets in the pouch and handed the wallet back to Sir Hubert. Both men looked at each other for some considerable time, saying nothing, but aware of a subtle change in the atmosphere of the interview.

"They're ration books, of course," Wade said presently. It was a statement made without inflexion, a mere registering act of recognition.

"Fifty million of them have been printed," Sir Hubert explained. "One of the biggest secret operations of all time. Not only in this country, but everywhere. America, Europe, Asia. All over the world there must be nearly two billion sets of basic ration books ready for distribution."

Wade shrugged helplessly. "But, Sir Hubert, why? What's it all about?"

Sir Hubert replaced the ration books on his desk and returned with a pale blue printed form which he handed to Wade. It appeared to be an official agreement of some kind with space at the bottom for a signature. Wade read it quickly, sensing in advance the meaning of the formal sentences. He glanced at Sir Hubert.

"If I sign this I take it I'm enrolled?" he said.

Sir Hubert nodded. "If you sign you accept unconditionally and without question the authority of the Bureau. You accept an absolute discipline, and you obey orders without question. In return we offer security for you and your family, and an eventual reunion with your wife and son when your period of duty is over."

"So that's the bargain," Wade said solemnly. "Loyalty in exchange for security." A pause, then: "Do you honestly believe things are going to be as bad as that?"

"Worse," said Sir Hubert quietly. "Much worse."

Wade pulled his fountain pen from his breast pocket.

"I'll sign," he said.

Wade spent the remainder of the day at Imperial Court. The pale blue form might have been a military recruiting form, so quickly and efficiently did the wheels begin to turn. Without saying anything further, Sir Hubert had passed him on to a Mr. Jaffe, a tall bony man with dreamy eyes, who asked innumerable questions and wrote the answers on a large folded form headed *Attestation*. By the time he had finished the form was virtually Wade's biography.

From there he was escorted by one of the elegant secretaries into the basement of the building, where surprisingly, there was a well-equipped clinic. Two doctors examined him with painstaking care, and X-rays were taken. Wade was just beginning to feel like a biological specimen on a microscope slide when he was told to dress.

He eyed the doctors questioningly, but they were uncommunicative. "Think I'll live?" he asked sardonically.

One of the doctors stared at him for a moment, without change of expression. He said: "Yes—if you call it living." He didn't bother to elaborate on his enigmatic statement, but went off into an adjacent room.

The other doctor came nearer and said, in confidential tones: "In the ordinary way and if I were a G.P. I'd give you the usual routine advice. You know—smoke less, lay off the drink. But those things don't matter any more, or rather, they won't matter very soon." Then, more quietly: "If you're fond of a smoke and a drink, you could do worse than lay in a stock."

Wade thought he saw what he meant, and said so.

The next process in the machinery of recruitment was a psychoneural examination during which an attractive mature woman in a white smock made recordings of his brain activity on an electroencephalograph. Looking her over as she adjusted the controls on the instrument, he decided that his brain waves would show a marked plus. It wasn't fair to the patient to employ glamour girls to make such tests, he thought. They ought to use dead-beats.

After that came a long and tiring question and answer session with an elderly psychiatrist. A microphone on the desk was connected to a tape-recorder on a small table to the rear, and Wade observed that the tape spools were rotating. Officialdom was certainly taking no chances with Philip Wade.

At ten minutes past five the machinery came to a halt; all examinations had been completed and Wade was conducted back to Sir Hubert's office. Sir Hubert eyed him speculatively, then waved him into a chair. He smiled without moving his lips.

"I suppose you've had enough of the routine, Mr. Wade?"

"I guess so."

"Never mind. I can assure you that it is necessary."

Wade pondered for a moment, then said: "I get the feeling that all this was predetermined—that you knew I'd sign, that you knew exactly how I'd react."

Sir Hubert allowed his hands to flutter vaguely. "We can't afford to take chances. We select our personnel in accordance with reliable psychological principles. If I had had any doubts whatever I should never have shown you those ration books."

"I still don't know what it all adds up to," Wade said resentfully. "My main feeling is—"

"I know," Sir Hubert interrupted. "You feel you've been—what is the expression?—railroaded..."

"Railroaded into a job I didn't ask for. What worries me is what I'm going to tell my wife. Are you serious about this Arctic evacuation business?"

"Absolutely serious. At this very moment a vast airlift is in operation, flying thousands of women and children to Zones D and E in the Arctic. Don't worry about the conditions, Mr. Wade. The Arctic camps are very up to date. Atomic reactors supply a communal heating system, and they are comfortable in a mildly austere way. I'll tell you this—your wife and son will be much happier in the Arctic than those who are left behind will be, and in not too many weeks."

"What exactly is going to happen, Sir Hubert?"

"You will be fully informed when your attestation papers are approved."

"When is that likely to be?"

"Tomorrow—probably in the afternoon."

"And what about my job as editor of *Outlook*?"

"It will cease, as from tomorrow."

Wade frowned and bit his lip. "Officially I'm supposed to give one month's notice…"

Sir Hubert smiled ironically. "Only one month? Mr. Holtz evidently doesn't value you as much as we do. However, you need not worry. The Bureau will deal with any problems arising from matters of contract."

"And so far as my wife and son are concerned, when would they be expected to—leave for the Arctic?"

Sir Hubert regarded him steadily. "Assuming your attestation papers are approved, they would leave, say, in three days."

Wade rocketed out of his chair, momentarily horrified. Sir Hubert waved a pacifying hand at him. "Four days, if you prefer it. Even a week. But time is getting short, and air reservations are becoming difficult. I strongly recommend you to leave the matter to me. It is more urgent than you imagine."

"*What* is more urgent?" Wade demanded. "That's all I want to know. You give me hints—insinuations. Rationing—water rationing—but why? And when?"

Sir Hubert shook his head slowly. "I'm sorry to have been so uninformative, Mr. Wade, but I, too, am bound by red tape and security. I have, unwisely perhaps, released to you a little more information that I ought to have done."

He paused, and crossed to the window, looking out at the busy road far below. "I have tried to impress on you the acute urgency of the situation, and you in turn must impress your wife in the same way."

"Supposing she refuses to leave?" Wade asked.

"You may find it a great handicap in the months to come, and the Bureau may decide not to use your services anyway. We must have individuals of independent character who, in effect, have no immediate and local ties."

Wade stood up, a little wearily. "All right, Sir Hubert. I'll do my best. I suppose you want me to talk to my wife today..."

"The sooner the better."

"Okay, I'll try—but I don't think it will work."

"It *will* work—provided you go home sober," said Sir Hubert brusquely.

Wade nodded doubtfully.

"I'll be contacting you tomorrow," Sir Hubert went on. "Meanwhile, don't be deceived by the normal appearance of the everyday world around you. It is a veneer that will soon be stripped off."

Wade shook hands with Sir Hubert and went home.

He did as Sir Hubert had suggested—he went home sober. Driving his car through Bayswater he became involved in an immense traffic jam. Completely immobilised, he became slowly aware of the reason for the traffic hold-up: an earth tremor was in progress, and the traffic lights about a hundred yards ahead had broken down, probably due to fracture of the underground wiring.

He was hardly aware of the movements of the earth; there was a subtle sense of vibration, and an elusive murmur of distant thunder. Somewhere remote, glass tinkled against stone. Presently impatience began to show itself in the truculent sounding of car horns on all sides, but he remained passively inactive, sitting relaxed in the driving seat, holding the wheel lightly. After some twenty minutes the traffic began to move again, and he observed that a police constable had taken over the duty of the paralysed traffic lights.

Funny how you got used to things, he thought. The way you got used to earthquakes and tremors. The way your mind adapted itself to new ideas and new concepts, and came to accept them without question. Sir Hubert was no longer an enigmatic individual overshadowing his future; he was already something real in the dead past, a fact of existence. And the threat that he suggested was hanging over humanity like a dark thundercloud had become an accepted component of life and living. All hell, it seemed, was about to break loose on an unsuspecting world that seemed to be much the same as usual—but what kind of hell?

You could add two and two together and make three, four or five. Ration books, for instance. There was going to be a shortage of the basic necessities of existence—even water. In fact, it looked as if water might be the key to the whole situation. What was it Shirley had said that time in the Globe? *Supposing the oceans did disappear... mightn't it introduce economic difficulties?... no imports... no exports... no grain ships, no oil tankers...*

But why no water? So long as there were rainclouds and rivers and springs there would always be water—or would there? Wade asked himself the question, but couldn't answer it. He pressed on the accelerator and made his way home.

He entered the house with a greater sense of proprietorship than usual, probably because he realised that to some extent the future of the house was a function of his own immediate future. It was a house destined to become deserted, desolated—not for any tangible reason that one could produce as evidence, but because of a number of correlated sinister events over the entire planet.

Janet was ironing, and she looked tired and pale. He kissed her formally.

"You're early, Phil," she said.

He made a murmur of agreement. "Where's David?"

"At Victor's home watching television."

He took off his coat and hung it up, then returned to the living room and lit a cigarette.

"I'll make some tea," Janet said, but he took her shoulders, restraining her.

He said quietly: "I spent all afternoon in a government department in Whitehall. I came straight home."

She glanced briefly at him but made no comment.

"I had an interview with Sir Hubert Piercey, followed by medical and psychological examinations. How would you like it if I were to become a government official?"

She turned to him, smiling. "I'd like it fine, but why should they pick you, Phil?"

"You never did believe Stenniger, did you?"

"Not very much."

"Well, he was on the level, Janet. Sir Hubert has me lined up for a job."

"What kind of a job?"

He shrugged. "I don't really know as yet. It had to do with information services, press liaison, censorship, and so on."

Janet returned to her ironing. "Funny kind of job, if you ask me. I mean, not knowing exactly what it amounts to. Did Sir Hubert mention salary?"

"It's unimportant. He said I could have whatever I asked, but it won't be worth anything in a few months."

"It will be worth something to *me*," she stated.

"That's just the point, my dear. This is more than the mere question of a job. It's a development of what you might call the world situation. New government departments are being set up, and there are all the indications of a powerful machinery being established—to control the population. The same thing is happening in other countries."

She looked at him seriously, not interrupting.

"Sir Hubert showed me something unbelievable this afternoon, Janet. Ration books. For food, fuel—and water. There's a big crisis coming up, and the government are taking steps to deal with it."

There was no incredulity in her expression—just calm, sober interest.

"I don't know the whole story, but I can make one or two intelligent guesses. It seems that I was pretty near to the truth when I wrote that *Outlook* feature on the Nutcracker H-bomb tests. The bed of the Pacific Ocean *was* fractured, and water is pouring into cavities inside the earth. Slowly enough, maybe, but at the same time fast enough to cause a significant fall in water level all over the world. In a few months most of the ports and harbours of the world are going to be useless. Shipping will be paralysed. And for a country like ours which depends so much on imports, that's a serious matter."

Janet nodded slowly; he had never known her so attentive.

"According to Sir Hubert things are going to be bad. He seems to think there will be a shortage of water as well as food, and things like coal and petrol and oil will be in short supply, which will mean that industry will grind to a halt."

"That's reasonable," she said quietly. "Naturally there would have to be a kind of Ministry of Information to put out reassuring propaganda—to try to make things seem better than they are."

"That would seem to be the general idea," Wade agreed.

"I think you'd better take the job, Phil," she said.

He finished his cigarette and flicked the stub into the grate. A minor detail of fact crystallised momentarily in his mind. If shipping became paralysed there would be no more tobacco imports and therefore no more cigarettes. It was a bleak thought.

"There's more to it yet, Janet," he said. "There are strings attached." He considered for a few seconds, seeking the proper words to express what was in his mind. "The government are anxious to safeguard their own personnel, and their families. They have a plan to evacuate close relatives of their officials—to a place of safety..."

"Where?"

"Well—they're building special camps with all facilities, and there'll be plenty of food and everything..."

"But where?"

"In the Arctic."

There was a strangeness in her eyes that he found unfamiliar. He said: "I've known about the camps in the Arctic for a long time. Antarctica too."

"You mean—that David and I are supposed to go to one of these—these Arctic camps—and leave you here alone."

"I'm afraid so, Janet."

She put her hands to her cheeks theatrically, regarding him solemnly. "And if I say no...?"

"Well—the chances are..."

"You won't get the job."

"It looks that way. Sir Hubert feels that I mightn't give of my best if my family were in danger."

"And if you don't get the job we'll all be in danger."

"Yes—according to the theory. That is, if you believe all this business about the coming crisis."

"It's not a question of believing it, Phil. No government would take steps like this unless there was a very real danger. I'm not worried about you or me—it's David I'm thinking of."

Wade lit up another cigarette. He felt the need to do something, to indulge in any mechanical activity, however trivial, in order to veil his astonishment at Janet's reaction. The stubborn opposition that he had anticipated had never materialised; instead, she had accepted all that he had said with an honest sincerity that seemed almost naïve. Feminine intuition, perhaps? At all events, Janet seemed to take the situation more seriously than he did. For some indefinable reason he felt gratified.

"When would we have to go?" Janet asked.

"Sir Hubert said in about three days."

"That doesn't leave much time."

"He said a big airlift was in operation and that reservations were getting difficult."

She seemed to sigh internally in some intimate and personal gesture of resignation. He wanted to go to her and hold her in his arms, and console her and reassure her, but he did nothing.

"When will you see Sir Hubert again?" she asked.

"Tomorrow afternoon."

She came towards him and put one hand gently on his shoulder. "I have to leave it to you, Phil. We're in your hands, David and I."

"It's *your* decision, Janet," he said firmly, but she shook her head.

"You're so wrong, Phil. Why don't you ever like to face up to responsibility? I'm your wife and David's your son and we'll do whatever you say."

He stood up, vaguely irritated, inhaling deeply on his cigarette. "Janet, we're not living in feudal times. You and I are individuals and I wouldn't want to dictate to you…"

"You've missed the point, Phil, as usual. Don't you see, all I know about any of this business is what you tell me? I'm taking you on trust. If you think Sir Hubert is right and that there is a real and terrible crisis on the way, then I'll do whatever you say."

"I don't know what to think," Wade said, and, indeed, he found himself curiously objective towards the entire situation. Did he really take Sir Hubert seriously? At any rate he had signed the recruitment paper, but—and here an uneasy misgiving trembled in his abdomen—it was always possible that he had signed in order to take the easy way out. Even Shirley had accused him of being weak. "I'll have to consider it," he added vaguely. "It will need a lot of thinking about."

"Don't think for too long, Phil," Janet said. "I know you're a good thinker, but sometimes you have to act too. And this might be one of those times."

Wade smiled sardonically and patted her cheek, but there was no sense of intimacy in the contact. "I'll try to pin Sir Hubert down tomorrow," he promised. "I'll get the facts, and then I'll know what to do." As an afterthought he added: "I think maybe he was exaggerating just a little. All this talk about Arctic camps is just a trifle melodramatic—perhaps to try and force my hand..."

Janet regarded him sadly. "Would he need to force your hand, Phil?"

He made no reply, despising himself for the hollowness of his words. What's the matter with me? he asked himself. I seem to cultivate indecision, to be on both sides of the fence at one and the same time. I *know* Sir Hubert is right and yet something inside me sneers at the thought, and I know Janet is sincere, but I play cat and mouse with her on a matter that might mean a choice of life or death. What's wrong with me for God's sake?

Janet said: "Since we may have only three days together, Phil, perhaps we ought to have a drink together."

"To celebrate?" he asked, hating himself the moment the words were uttered.

She seemed to shrink inside herself. "No, not to celebrate. I—I just thought we might try to have fun while there's still time."

Wade relented and embraced her clumsily. "I'm sorry, Janet—so help me I am. I'm confused. So many things seem to be happening and I'm not sure I've made sense of anything yet."

"You've never been any other way," she said simply.

"We'll have a drink," he said. "I'll run up to the off-licence in the car. We'll drink a toast to Sir Hubert."

"To each other," said Janet.

And on the way to the off-licence he found himself whistling happily. It might have been a sober evening, but as things had turned out—well, the world was all right again. You're on the beam, brother. First right and second left. It's a wonderful world when it's seventy-proof, come earthquake, come drought, come famine, come fire...

He drove on into the descending night.

V

THE NEXT DAY THINGS BEGAN TO MOVE. IT WAS AS IF INVISible forces had been at work overnight, severing the ties that held him secure in the present. Willis, for instance, was sitting in his office when he arrived, sitting at Wade's own desk, dictating letters to Betty. He looked up when Wade entered, and grinned foolishly.

"Sorry, Phil," he said apologetically. "I seem to be promoted, or something."

"Congratulations," Wade said, with irony. "What do I do? Sit on the floor?"

"Holtz wants to see you. He came in early—around eight-thirty. First thing I knew he'd ordered me to take over the editorship of *Outlook*."

Wade eyed the other man thoughtfully, but said nothing.

"He looked worried," Willis continued. "What have you been up to, Phil?"

"When I find out, I'll tell you."

Wade went to see Holtz. He was sitting at Stenniger's old desk, surrounded by paper, and writing meticulously with a cheap ball pen on a sheet of quarto paper. He smiled at Wade and waved him into a chair.

"Good morning, Mr. Wade," Holtz said pleasantly. "I suppose I ought to be angry with you, but I am not a man who angers easily."

"Anything wrong, Mr. Holtz?" Wade asked.

Holtz stood up and crossed to the window, turning his back on Wade. "I'm rather disappointed in you. I was relying on you to remain with us, to guide the destiny of *Outlook* in the future as you have done in the past. Consequently you will realise that it was rather a shock to me when Sir Hubert Piercey telephoned me at my home last night."

He turned to face Wade, and there was accusation in his eyes.

Wade shrugged his shoulders. "Until yesterday I didn't know a thing about it, Mr. Holtz, so help me. Only vague hearsay and rumours. Even now I don't know for certain..."

"Sir Hubert seemed very certain. He asked me—indeed, he instructed me—to release you forthwith. I only hope you are doing the right thing, Mr. Wade. I had high hopes of you. With this organisation your future could have been very bright."

"What exactly did Sir Hubert say?"

"Is there any need for me to explain? Yesterday you were interviewed and examined for some important but undefined government post, and you have been accepted."

"I haven't been notified as yet."

"No doubt you will be. Sir Hubert asked me to waive the customary month's notice of resignation. He may have very good reasons, but it still leaves this company in a difficult position. On a monthly periodical it wouldn't be quite so important, but on a weekly... I've appointed Willis as editor pending an official appointment. I hope he is competent."

"He's competent enough," Wade pronounced wearily.

"Then there's nothing more to be said, Mr. Wade. Under the circumstances we can hardly pay you a month's salary..."

Wade put up an arm. "I understand, Mr. Holtz. But look here—I've heard nothing definite from Sir Hubert. So far as I'm concerned nothing has changed..."

"But it has," Holtz insisted. "*Outlook* has a new editor as from this morning. Good-bye, Mr. Wade."

Wade left the office angrily. Sir Hubert had been too damned high-handed, he thought. It was one thing to make the offer of a job, but quite another to sabotage an existing job—a good enough job at that. He went to his own office and, ignoring Willis, lifted the phone and dialled the operator.

"Get me Sir Hubert Piercey at the International Bureau of Information at Imperial Court in Whitehall Crescent," he said.

Thirty seconds later he was talking to Sir Hubert.

"Philip Wade here," he announced aggressively. "I've just been talking to Mr. Holtz…"

"Excellent!" Sir Hubert's voice was remote and resonant over the line. "So you know all about it."

"All I know is that things have been happening behind my back."

It seemed to Wade that Sir Hubert chuckled. "Perhaps our methods are somewhat unconventional, but don't let it worry you, Mr. Wade. Naturally I had to take steps to ensure that you would be available immediately, and that meant going over your head, direct to Holtz. I've just had the attestation report in from the security people. You're in, Mr. Wade. As from now you're a government employee."

Wade hesitated, uncertain as to how he ought to react. "Well," he said reluctantly, "I think it's high-handed to say the least. Supposing I'd decided to decline your offer?"

"You can't, Mr. Wade. You signed a document, remember. It happens to be legally binding."

"So what am I supposed to do next?"

"You are to report to a Colonel Brindle at Room Five in the Consort Building in Kingsway. He will assume responsibility for you from now on."

"When am I supposed to see this Colonel Brindle?"

"As soon as you are ready. Now, if you like."

"Very well," Wade said reluctantly. "I'll go there now."

He hung up and eyed Willis solemnly.

"Best of luck, Pete," he murmured.

Willis grinned boyishly. "Well, thanks. But what's it all about, Phil? Have you been fired?"

"No. I—I've seen the light—got the message—been sent—however you like to put it. Frankly I'm not at all sure what it's all about, but one thing's certain—you've got yourself an editorial chair. I hope it lasts a long time."

"You sound as if you don't think it will..."

"I'm sure it will—as long as civilisation itself lasts."

Willis regarded him questioningly, but Wade made an enigmatic face and pushed his hands deep into his pockets.

"I've got things to do," he said. "I'll be back some time to pick up a few personal belongings. Meanwhile..."

Willis raised his eyebrows in surprise. "On the level, Phil? You're really leaving?"

"I've already left," Wade said sourly.

On the way out of the building he looked in on Shirley Sye, but she wasn't in her office. Walking slowly down the stairs he encountered her secretary, who was coming up with an armful of folders.

"Mrs. Sye around?" he enquired.

The girl shook her head, peering at him through butterfly-framed spectacles. "She's gone over to the Dorchester, Mr. Wade. The Brunot spring collection is being modelled."

"Never mind," Wade said. "I'll see her some other time."

Going out of the main entrance he paused, and looked back. The old familiar foyer with its flatwashed walls and peeling paint;

the antiquated elevator and the stairway leading down to the washrooms and lavatories—and even as he looked MacLaren came into view, climbing the stairs with unsteady precision, with the inevitable home-rolled cigarette drooping from his lips.

"Hello, dear boy," said MacLaren, waving a hand.

"Hi, Mac," Wade called, then went quickly out into Fleet Street, not anxious to become involved in conversation.

He walked the full length of the street towards Aldwych and Kingsway, not minding the rain, looking around him with eyes that held more than a hint of melancholy. Moving out of Fleet Street was like emigrating, and he was conscious of a deep emotional wrench. At Chancery Lane, however, the mood began to pass off, and by the time he had walked beyond the Law Courts his mind had turned towards the future, and there was a certain jauntiness in his movements, and Fleet Street was behind him in both time and space.

Seven minutes later he entered the Consort Building in Kingsway.

From the outside the Consort Building resembled any ordinary office block, with rows of steel-framed rectangular windows rising six storeys above the street. At ground level was a parade of large plate-glass windows in which were displayed a variety of domestic electrical products such as refrigerators, washing machines, spin dryers, convector heaters and so on. A narrow bronze fascia above the windows announced: *Electrical and Allied Appliance Company, Limited*. At one time, Wade recalled, this had indeed been the head office of one of Britain's biggest electrical manufacturing groups, but the window displays were all that remained. The interior of the building had been taken over by the government.

He had not walked more than four paces into the spacious entrance hall when he was intercepted by a uniformed guard who looked him up and down without compassion.

"Mr. Philip Wade to see Colonel Brindle in Room Five," Wade stated cheerfully.

The guard said nothing, but merely pointed to a recessed booth in one wall labelled *Enquiries*.

"Thanks," murmured Wade. He went over to the booth and found himself staring at a pretty brunette in a neat grey costume. He repeated what he had said to the guard.

"Mr. Philip Wade," she echoed, referring to a check list. "Oh yes, Mr. Wade. The Colonel is expecting you. If you will wait a moment I'll have you escorted."

She pressed a white button on the counter. Ten seconds later another guard appeared from an adjacent door.

"Mr. Wade for Colonel Brindle," said the brunette.

Wade followed the guard across the entrance hall to beyond the elevator and down a wide corridor at the end of which was a double door. At the other side of the door was a carpeted staircase leading downwards, then another double door, and another corridor. Finally the guard stopped outside a glass-panelled door bearing the legend: *Colonel Brindle—Chief of Intelligence Division—International Bureau of Information*.

The guard tapped on the door and went in. A moment later he reappeared and nodded briefly at Wade.

Wade went into the office.

It was a large office, without windows, flooded with light from half a dozen grilled fluorescents hanging from the high ceiling. The walls were grey and covered with a patchwork of large maps, and some of the maps were peppered with little coloured flags. At one end of the room was a big square table with another map on it, and at the other end another table with two teleprinters, one of which was clicking merrily away to itself and pushing paper intermittently from its roller.

Colonel Brindle's desk was set midway between the two tables—a long and imposing desk with a glass top, supporting an unreasonable quantity of telephones and intercom switchboard units. And behind this mass of communications equipment sat the Colonel himself—in sober civilian clothes, Wade was surprised to note. He was a tall angular man, poised uncomfortably on his swivel chair, with thin greying hair, a long sad jaw, and a pair of the bluest eyes Wade had ever seen. He stood up as Wade came in, leaning stiffly across the desk and extending a long arm.

Wade shook hands firmly, noting that the Colonel had fingers of steel.

"Good of you to get here so soon," said Brindle in a voice that sounded too gentle for the big bony body from which it came. "Sit down."

Wade sat down facing the Colonel.

"I won't waste time," Brindle went on. "As from this moment you are working for me, and you're not likely to see anything more of Sir Hubert Piercey. Your official status here is Deputy Intelligence Officer. You'll be immediately responsible to Major Carey, but you won't see much of him because he'll be travelling round a great deal. There will be more documents for you to sign to make the whole thing watertight..." He broke off and moved his lips into what resembled the shape of a grin. "And watertight is the precise word, believe me, Wade."

Wade nodded. There didn't seem to be anything to say.

"You'll be on open salary—which means you can draw what

you like each week, within limits. We don't want you to go buying half a dozen Jaguars, naturally, but we want you to have everything you need. In this kind of job money is a very minor consideration."

"I see."

"You'll have an office overlooking the Intelligence Filter Room. That's the nerve centre of this building. We have radio-teleprinter links with every corner of the world, and every link is jammed with signal traffic. All signals are encoded. You'll act in close liaison with the Code and Cypher Division."

"Fine—but what exactly do I have to do?" Wade asked.

"You'll get full instructions later. Generally, you will do much the same kind of job as you've been doing in Fleet Street. You'll assess the value and significance of all incoming signals, and integrate them into one comprehensive picture of the world situation."

"You mean—like fitting the pieces into a jig-saw?"

"More or less. We think you'll be good at that kind of work. You did it pretty effectively in the pages of *Outlook*."

"Well—thanks."

"You'll also be responsible for releasing news to the press and public broadcasting channels—only it won't be news, it will be propaganda designed to maintain the national morale."

"So it's *that* kind of crisis?"

Colonel Brindle stood up and crossed to one of the wall maps, beckoning Wade to follow him. Wade went over to the map. Brindle was pointing to a large blue expanse that was obviously the Pacific Ocean.

"Right here," he said in a matter-of-fact tone of voice, "is a fracture in the ocean bed, centred on Kaluiki. We've been able to make some measurements, in between earthquakes. The fracture is about two thousands miles long and it gets bigger every day."

He stared bleakly at Wade. "It's an automatic cycle. As the water pours into cavities beneath the ocean bed it causes cooling of the hot interior. The resulting contractions combined with steam pressure blow open further cracks, and so it goes on."

"You mean—it will never stop?"

"Only when there isn't any more water left to pour through the cracks. In other words—when the oceans have run dry."

For a moment Wade found himself at a loss for words. Presently he said: "But is that likely to happen? Seriously, I mean."

"Inside three months. Probably less."

"But sea level is only dropping very slowly…"

"Was," Brindle stated emphatically. "There has been an alarming increase in the rate since the earthquakes in the western hemisphere. We haven't been able to make a complete investigation, but we believe the Pacific shocks have opened up a structural flaw in the bed of the Atlantic."

"If that is true…"

"If it's true we can expect more and more earthquakes on both sides of the world, and the water will drain away more and more rapidly. According to the latest measurements and statistics, it has already started. Sea level is down by more than ten feet. There are only two ports in these islands capable of accepting shipping of more than ten-thousand tons displacement. By the end of next week it will be down by twenty feet, perhaps more, and a week or two later you'll be able to walk to France if you feel so inclined."

"I can see," Wade said solemnly, "that this is going to be a serious matter for everyone."

Brindle shaped his lips again into one of his rare ironic smiles. "That is probably the understatement of all time. You may not realise it yet, Wade, but mankind is about to fight his most violent and vicious rearguard action. There can only be a few survivors, and they'll be the lucky ones who can get to the polar regions."

"You mean—because of the water?"

"Exactly. If the oceans go, there will be no more rain, because rain is simply water vapour evaporated from the ocean surface. No rain means no clouds, and that means a hot dry summer. Lakes and rivers will dry out—for ever. There will be an end to agriculture and an end to livestock—except in the Arctic and Antarctic where there is plenty of water for tens of thousands of years, in the form of ice."

"I think I see the whole picture now," Wade said. "At least, all the disconnected pieces seem to tie up."

"There are a lot more pieces that you and I haven't even thought of yet." Brindle returned to his desk, and Wade to his chair. They sat down.

"Have they evacuated your family yet?" Brindle asked.

Wade shook his head.

"Better not delay too long. The situation is likely to explode overnight. I'll ring Sir Hubert and fix it."

"When?"

"You mean when will your family be leaving? Tomorrow, I hope. I'll do my best."

Wade pondered unhappily for a few seconds. "And what about us, Colonel? The people who are left behind?"

"Those who are left behind fall into two categories. The government officials, such as you and I, with the support of the police and the armed forces, will try to maintain law and order for as long as possible. There will have to be stringent rationing fairly administered. We shall be among the administrators. But in the end there will be a complete breakdown of civilisation, and humanity will revert back to the law of the survival of the fittest. Before that happens we shall pull out and join our families in the Arctic bases."

"And the second category?"

"The mass of the people. Those who are going to die, inevitably, before the year is out."

"Then—what's the point of trying to maintain law and order. Why not pull out now...?"

Brindle stroked his nose thoughtfully. "That would hardly be either humanitarian or ethical, though I imagine the abstract graces will go by the board very quickly, in any case. No, Wade, we have to keep control over the situation because there is always the possibility that someone will find a solution to the problem. Scientists all over the world are trying to devise economical ways of pumping the water back from the sub-oceanic cavities, or laying pipelines to carry water from the polar regions to the civilised zones, or even synthesising water from hydrogen and oxygen. With a tremendous technological effort it might be possible to pull the rabbit out of the hat in time."

"I hope to God they can do it," said Wade earnestly.

"We can only wait and see. Incidentally, if it's any consolation to you, you will be one of the first to know. In fact, you'll be the first to know about anything, with the exception of the code and cypher staff."

"That makes me a happy man," Wade said sardonically.

"And now," Brindle announced, "I'll take you to your office and introduce you to some of the people you will be working with."

Wade followed the other man out of the room.

The Intelligence Filter Room was a further two floors below ground and was either a converted basement, or, and this seemed more likely to Wade, a recent and purposeful extension to the building. The room had a functional appearance, as if it had been designed from first principles expressly for communications purposes.

Wade was only able to glance quickly around as he followed Brindle to a steel staircase leading up to a balcony. He was among teleprinters, about forty of them arranged in orderly rows, and beyond them was a long switchboard with tiny flashing lights. There were girls and men operating the machines and supervising the switchboard. Behind the clatter of the keyboards he thought he could detect the faint whine of air conditioning plant; the atmosphere of the room was certainly cool and fresh.

The balcony, which extended all round the teleprinter room, was lined with doors and windows. Some of the windows were large, like shop fronts, reminding him of the control rooms in a television studio. People moved behind the windows, engaged in their own assigned activities.

They went into a door labelled *Intelligence*, and here was an ante-room with two girls and desks and typewriters and filing cabinets. In the far wall a metal door bore the sign: NO UNAUTHORISED ADMISSION. Colonel Brindle pressed a red-topped button recessed into the wall, and the door slid silently to one side. They went through. A moment later the door closed behind them.

This was a short corridor, with two doors on either side. All the doors were labelled. To the right he saw *Code and Cypher Department*, and, further on, *Lieutenant Patten—Code and Cypher Officer*. On the left the first door announced *Major Carey—Intelligence Officer*, and on the second door was *Philip Wade—Deputy Intelligence Officer*. They went into his office.

It was a nice office—big and airy, with cool blue walls and a pure white ceiling with strip lights. The desk was cubic and modern, but not too much so. There were three telephones, black, white and green. The carpet was a regulation brown, but soft enough to sleep on. An enormous safe with a combination lock was built solidly into one wall, and a row of filing cabinets with ostentatious locks adorned another. There were maps too, with little flags, but they had not been positioned.

Brindle eyed Wade quizzically. "Satisfactory?"

"Excellent."

He indicated a small intercom unit on the desk. "If you want a stenographer, or want to call the Cypher Officer, or Major Carey, or me—or if you just want coffee—use this."

"Do I have a secretary?" Wade asked.

"Sorry, no secretary. In a department like yours we can't afford to have too many people with inside knowledge. It's virtually a one-man job. Security reasons."

"I understand."

"All right," said Brindle. "We'll move on."

They returned to the corridor and entered the door with the sign *Lieutenant Patten—Code and Cypher Officer*. It was an office similar to his own, Wade observed, with a built-in safe and a bank of filing cabinets with large locks, but this office had been inhabited for some time, and the desk was untidy with papers and books.

Patten was a lean, bespectacled man, tall, but not so tall as Wade, with blond hair that bore the hint of a wave. He wore a faded grey suit and a Royal Air Force tie, but that was the only concession made to uniform. Wade wondered vaguely about the military titles of Patten and Brindle, but decided that they were wearing civilian clothes for some obscure reason of security. On the other hand he was unable to reconcile Patten's army rank of

Lieutenant with the Air Force tie. He dismissed the matter with a mental shrug, and concentrated on the man himself.

"Glad to meet you, Wade," Patten said affably. "Things have been difficult with Major Carey being away so much. From now on everything should go smoothly."

"I hope you're right," Wade remarked.

Brindle said: "Lieutenant Patten has been handling a considerable amount of the intelligence side out of sheer necessity. He'll be able to show you the ropes."

"Only too pleased," Patten smiled.

"Your only means of contact with the communication network will be through the Cypher Office," Brindle went on. "All incoming and outgoing signals pass through Lieutenant Patten, or, in his absence, the chief cypher clerk, Miss Vance."

"I understand," Wade said.

"I'll leave you here now," said Brindle. "You and Patten will probably have a lot to talk about."

"Okay, Colonel."

Brindle left, and for a few moments Patten and Wade eyed each other with a certain reserve: it wasn't quite embarrassment, but rather the preliminary unconscious groping of two strangers for some point of psychic contact. Wade produced his cigarettes, and Patten accepted with a little too much gratitude. They lit up.

Patten glanced quickly at an old-fashioned pocket watch, then looked brightly at Wade. "It's nearly twelve. Tell you what. I'll show you the main Cypher Office and introduce you to Miss Vance, then what say we pop out for a beer and a bite?"

"Fine," said Wade, mentally substituting several whiskies for the beer.

"That way we can talk informally and I can put you in the picture as to the set-up here."

Patten led the way into the Cypher Office. Not much to see: a big, austere room—two built-in safes—four large tables—four girls—curious machines that resembled oversized typewriters but were obviously some kind of mechanical coding device—and the inevitable filing cabinets.

"This is Miss Vance," said Patten.

Wade looked at Miss Vance. She was pert and attractive, with dark hair, rather short, and the suggestion of a fringe, and deep brown intelligent eyes. No cosmetics that you could notice, but a clear, youthful complexion that needed no enhancement. She wasn't beautiful and she wasn't glamorous, Wade thought, but she had that indefinite something, that mysterious feminine magnetism, that came over without artifices and without gimmicks. She dressed plainly, in black with a high white collar. The way she smiled was subtle, and she smiled with her eyes as well as her lips.

"How do you do," Miss Vance said correctly, in a voice that was a delight to listen to.

Twenty-five—or perhaps twenty-six, Wade estimated. Almost young enough to be his own daughter. He broke through the spell of fascination that seemed to be binding him and inclined his head in a formal gesture.

"I regard Miss Vance as my deputy," said Patten. "She knows as much about the cypher side as I do—probably more. Once you've settled in you'll probably be seeing more of her than you will of me."

And that might be something to look forward to, Wade thought. He said: "I'm sure Miss Vance is most efficient and I imagine I'll be relying on her a great deal in due course."

"I'm sure you will," Patten remarked.

The girl smiled, and some polite crosstalk followed, and then Wade and Patten left the office and made their way towards the outside world.

By the end of the afternoon Wade felt that he had the whole business taped. Maybe the impending crisis was as serious as Colonel Brindle had implied, maybe not; whatever the truth of the matter the world was taking it seriously. There had been, during the past six months, innumerable secret talks on an international basis and at top level, facilitated through the existing mechanism of the United Nations. For the first time in the history of mankind the nations of the world had agreed upon a common policy to deal with the situation. At present this policy was in an embryonic stage; vital channels of communication were being established, and the world was being encompassed by a comprehensive network of communication links, based principally upon the radioteleprinter, which was considered to be the most secure means of transmission.

In effect it was a pooling of the world's brains for the benefit of mankind—or a portion of mankind. Each country felt that it was essential to know in detail what was happening in every other part of the world. An international crisis committee had been set up, under the auspices of the United Nations, to consider difficulties as they arose. All this was top secret, of course, and no mention of it ever filtered into the public news services.

Significant, too, was the immense communal effort involved in the establishment of the polar bases. Every nation was participating, without counting the cost, doing their utmost within the limits of their individual economic capabilities. It had been tacitly recognised that the basic problem was one of survival, and it rather looked as if survival would only be possible in the regions of permanent ice.

The only disquieting note, from Wade's point of view, was the manner in which the facility for survival was being shared among the human race as a whole. It seemed to him that a ruthless form of selection had been adopted. The inhabitants of the polar evacuation camps were, so far as he could determine, government employees, or the families of government employees, and people of direct importance to the survival drive, such as scientists and technicians and chemists and doctors. The rest of the human race didn't seem to matter. He supposed that in a situation of this type one had to be ruthless; there had to be the governing class which knew the truth, and the outsiders who were fed with reassuring propaganda to sustain them to the terrible end.

That's how it was. Facts were facts, and a man had to accept the facts and make the best of them. He had been lucky, thanks, perhaps, to Stenniger's influence. Hard luck on people like Shirley Sye, but it was a hard world, and going to get even harder in the near future.

I'll make a success of this job, he told himself as he was driving home. I'll send Janet and David to the Arctic, and I'll join them in a few months. And if the crisis is solved before then, well—why worry? We shall get back to normal anyway.

After his first day in the International Bureau of Information Wade felt smugly pleased with the turn of events. Fortunately he was unable to see the future.

VI

JANET AND DAVID LEFT TWO DAYS LATER. IT WAS A QUIET, restrained parting, with no tears or sentiment, and in a way rather formal. The Arctic airlift planes, an assorted fleet of four-engined and jet passenger and freight aircraft, were based at High Waltham airfield some thirty miles to the west of London. Wade drove his family over early in the morning and they had lunch in the airfield canteen.

High Waltham was an ex-wartime airfield, built by the Royal Air Force to provide adequate runway facilities for heavy bombers. After the war it had been taken over by the Ministry of Civil Aviation as a stand-by landing ground and as a test zone for jet prototypes, but during latter years it had fallen into disuse—until the recent crisis.

Wade noted the signs of applied security—the new wire fence, eight feet tall, around the perimeter of the field, and the armed sentries patrolling inside the wire. There was only one entrance, with a large check post of new brick, where his documents were scrutinised by uniformed officials. At the reception building further examination and interrogation took place, after which he was informed that his wife and son had been assigned to flight thirty-six, scheduled to take off in eighty minutes. Time for a meal and a drink and a final good-bye.

And all too soon that good-bye was in the here and now, and he was kissing Janet for the last time and squeezing his son's shoulder and exchanging the last unpremeditated and banal words.

"Take good care of yourself, honey. And look after Davey for me."

"We'll be all right, Phil. It's you I'm worried about."

"Not to worry—I'll be okay, and I'll be coming up there to join you very soon."

"How soon, I wonder…"

"Two months, three months…"

"Phil, I don't want to say this, but…"

"You don't have to say anything, Janet. You ought to know better. I've been a reformed character for years."

"I trust you, Phil—but not when you drink too much."

"Then stop worrying. From what I've heard there won't be any drink left in the country in a few weeks."

"I don't know. It's hard to believe. The whole thing seems like a dream…"

Behind them the Tannoy system spoke in metallic tones. "Flight thirty-six. Flight thirty-six. Passengers for Flight thirty-six are asked to join their aircraft now, please. Take-off in four minutes."

People were walking over to the aircraft at the end of the long runway and mounting the stepped gangway. The sky was overcast, a dull uniform grey mottled with crawling raincloud, but the ground was dry. Wade watched silently as his wife and son joined the group of receding passengers, watched them as they climbed the gangway, pausing at the top to turn and wave, and continued to watch after they had disappeared into the comparative darkness of the fuselage.

Minutes ticked by, and then the four engines burst into noisy, vibrant life. Slowly the huge aircraft crept forward, turning into the line of the runway. And then the roar of power throbbed in his ears and flight thirty-six was a diminishing shape moving towards a remote vanishing point, and presently it was a tiny silhouette against the leaden sky.

When the aircraft had disappeared from view, Wade returned to his car and drove back to London. There was no positive reaction in his mind, merely a numb blankness and a vague sense of loss. But, curiously, as he entered the outer suburbs of the vast sprawling city, a certain feeling of exhilaration seeped into his veins. At first he resisted it, and tried to analyse it, but in the end he confessed that the feeling was perfectly natural. Why shouldn't a guy feel exultant when his family had been flown to safety, when they were secure from whatever horrors the future might bring?

But that wasn't the real reason, he told himself in a sudden mood of cynicism. The truth was that he had acquired a sense of freedom that was already changing his perspective of life. His wife and child were safe, it was true, but already far away, and he was a free agent in an unsettled and unpredictable world.

The spirit of adventure, he told himself. To be a lone wolf once more and face whatever is to come. But the thoughts were hollow and false. Adventure had nothing to do with it: the thing that was taking hold of his mind was the subtle anticipation of uninhibited, liberty and self-indulgence.

In this confused and self-critical frame of mind, Wade returned to his new office at the Consort Building in Kingsway.

Within a few days he realised, from the nature of the signal messages that passed through his hands, the ominous state of the world. Previously his information had been confined to censored press releases and hearsay, but now he was confronted from minute to minute with statistics and indisputable facts. Unpublishable facts.

The Pacific Ocean, for instance, had become unnavigable, due to powerful currents and enormous whirlpools covering an area of more than a million square miles. The Japanese islands had been utterly devastated by earthquakes and isolated by the seething ocean, and air relief was hopelessly inadequate. Sporadic signals from the Far East gave sparse details of rioting and bloodshed under conditions of famine and chaos. In China, on the eastern seaboard, things were little better, and even Australia had suffered considerably from the overall catastrophe.

The west coast of America, Wade learned, had also suffered to such an extent that in certain areas, Los Angeles and San Francisco included, martial law was the order of the day, and a security barrier had been laid down west of the Rockies to prevent panic-stricken movement of the population towards the east.

The terrestrial sea level had dropped by fourteen feet, and the rate of fall was accelerating swiftly. Already shipping was becoming paralysed on an international scale. The Suez Canal was rapidly becoming impassable and the majority of the major ports of the world were virtually unapproachable. Shipping had become the victim of a creeping paralysis, and the paralysis was killing vital imports and exports. Oil, grain, timber, newsprint, meat, metals, raw materials of all kinds, were rapidly becoming in short supply, and in some cases national stocks were less than two weeks. Despite the normal appearance of the everyday world, it was obvious to Wade that the storm was about to break any moment of any day.

It broke in a small way four days after the departure of Janet and David. The government took over all broadcasting services. The move was in no way ostentatious, taking the form of a behind-the-scenes seizure of power at executive level. An emergency broadcasting committee was formed to supervise and reshape, where necessary, all programmes, and, at the same time, the various services were telescoped into a single radio channel and a single television channel, covering the country in a nationwide network.

This was obviously the first step in the establishment of an effective propaganda blanket. Since there were now no alternative channels of radio and television entertainment, the audience was captive at all times. The change was noted briefly in the press as a "short-term measure designed to keep the public fully informed during temporary difficulties arising from the recent series of sporadic earth tremors in the Western Hemisphere".

But the earth tremors were by no means recent; they were continuing and, if anything, increasing in frequency. The seismic centre was far away, in mid-Atlantic, where, according to confidential reports, sub-oceanic activity of considerable violence was taking place, though not on the same drastic scale as in the Pacific. Europe and the east coast of America trembled periodically as the shock waves, tearing through the ocean bed, reached the continental land masses in attenuated form, but occasionally, resulting from some major cataclysm beneath the Atlantic, the recurrent trembling would suddenly burst into the terrifying reality of a full-scale earthquake. It was impossible to predict just where the peak force of the blow would strike. Depending, presumably, on the geological structure of the earth's crust in relation to the precise location of the seismic point of origin, the zones of maximum destruction occurred at random—in London one day, Glasgow another, or in Paris or Budapest or Casablanca.

The earthquakes, therefore, provided a reasonable and logical excuse for taking the broadcasting services under governmental control. Very few people realised that the real crisis was something much more insidious.

Wade, understanding all this, found himself wondering what the next step would be. The introduction of rationing, perhaps? It had to come—probably within a few days. Rationing, and then what? Nothing more—just the waiting and waiting while the oceans of the world ran dry and the scientists desperately sought a solution to the problem. A simple view of an unimaginable future, Wade thought. Probably far too simple.

He had overlooked one thing, and it happened two days later. The government, in one comprehensive edict, took over the control of all printing and publishing, and forthwith suppressed every newspaper and magazine in the land. In place of the wide variety of papers and periodicals that had formerly existed there was now only one daily news-sheet, entitled *National Express*, and one illustrated weekly, named *Comment*, both edited and produced under stringent governmental control.

The reason for this unprecedented and astonishing measure was announced in radio and television news bulletins. "Because of the temporary dislocation of shipping resulting from unexpectedly low spring tides, and the need to use all available freight space for essential commodities, imports of newsprint and bulk paper have been discontinued. During the period of the emergency, in an effort to conserve existing paper stocks, all publication and printing will be suspended with the exception of one four-page national newspaper and a small weekly magazine of illustrated comment. The government hope to restore normal publishing facilities as soon as it becomes possible to resume paper imports."

Wade thought it unlikely that the public would swallow the "low spring tides" part of the statement, and during the ensuing days he listened carefully to snatches of stray conversations that went on around him in public houses and restaurants, but there was little discernible reaction. A few people grumbled, others casually remarked that they thought things must be pretty bad, some decided it was time for a change of government, and there was an overall tendency to regard the entire thing as political in origin. Wade overheard a typical conversation in a saloon bar in High Holborn where two middle-aged labourers in tatty raincoats were imbibing from pint tankards of ale and smoking slim home-rolled cigarettes.

"The way I sees it, Ned, the Tories is lookin' arter their own interests."

"They always did, Bert."

"They knows damn well it was those H-bomb tests what started all this earthquake business, and they also knows that the workin' classes aren't going to put up with it much longer."

"Don't see as how the working classes can do much about the earthquakes."

"We can get 'em *out*, Ned. Give Labour a crack of the whip. That's what they're afraid of, ain't it?"

"Haven't heard as how the Labour Party is doing anything about it, Bert."

"That's just the point. You and me don't know what's going on in Parliament. Censorship's behind it, and this country is turning into a ruddy dictatorship, mark my words. The Tories is running the press now, with only one paper and a magazine, and the wireless and telly too."

"I still don't see as how we can do anything."

"A strike, Ned. A ruddy big general strike. Everyone out. That'd bring the bastards to their knees."

Ned grunted conditional approval and concentrated on his ale.

It illustrated, Wade thought, the universal ignorance of the real situation. Party politics had been dead for months; the political parties were functioning as an unofficial coalition government, and the Prime Minister had, weeks before, reconstituted the Cabinet to admit representatives of the Socialist and Liberal parties.

He wondered idly about the paper and newsprint situation. True, all imports had ceased, but stock levels in the country were more than adequate to permit a limited amount of publishing on a ration basis. On the other hand, if you took the long-term view, it was obvious that sooner or later all paper stocks would inevitably become exhausted, even if a widespread salvage and recovery scheme were instituted. Better to have one newspaper for a long time than plenty of papers and magazines for only a few weeks.

The first issue of the new, austere *National Express* was on sale the day after the announcement of the new arrangements. It was priced at one shilling.

During the first week at Consort Building Wade was too immersed in his work to make more than superficial contact with his colleagues. His visitors in the main were clerks from the Cypher Office, or Miss Vance herself, bringing decodes of incoming signals. Occasionally Colonel Brindle came in to check on progress, and one day Major Carey introduced himself, exchanged brisk conversation for about five minutes, then dashed off again on another mysterious mission out of London. Carey's visit was so brief and hurried that Wade afterwards remembered little of the man, retaining in his mind a vague image of a jovial, red-faced giant loosely wrapped in fawn tweeds.

During the lunch breaks Wade invariably sought out the nearest pub, following his habitual routine of plenty to drink and little to eat. Sometimes he was accompanied by Patten, but it soon became evident that Patten was not a drinking man, and preferred to eat in the more orthodox surroundings of a restaurant. Wade made no attempt to adapt himself to the other man's routine, but pursued his own way of life with a single-minded stubbornness.

Once or twice he thought he would walk down Fleet Street and lunch at the Globe, or perhaps even call in at the Stenniger building to find out what had happened since the arbitrary suppression of all publishing, but in the end he never strayed beyond Kingsway. At the back of his mind was the idea that he might encounter Shirley Sye. He had thought about Shirley quite a lot since Janet's departure, particularly during the long dark evenings, and one day, he promised himself, he would get in touch with her. But a casual accidental meeting would look better, with no suspicion of motivation. He smiled to himself at the word—his confused motivations of the night of Stenniger's party seemed incredible in retrospect, and he knew there would be less confusion next time, if there ever was a next time.

Quite by chance, one lunch time, he left the building with Miss Vance and walked down Kingsway with her towards Aldwych. It was a fine day, one of the few dry days of the year so far, and the sun was shining warmly through a faint haze of striated cloud. Wade bought a copy of the *National Express* and briefly scanned the headlines, recognising one of his own manufacture. *Coastal Silt may be Cultivated*, it announced, and, beneath: *Bold Plan to Boost Grain Crops*. The story, illustrated by a half-tone picture of a not too vast area of sand and silt exposed by the receding coastal waters, was based on a news story that he had dreamed up the day before—a quite impracticable plan to convert the increasing zones of silt and sand around the coast into fertile and arable land to offset impending scarcity of grain imports.

Miss Vance glanced briefly at the headline and said:

"Fiction, I take it?"

He nodded. "It comes under the heading of morale boosting."

"Do you really think people are going to believe that kind of thing?"

"It doesn't matter whether they do or not. The point is—it fills the front page with an optimistic story. The man in the street is looking for crisis news, but instead we give him pleasant dreams."

"Do you think it is fair?"

"I haven't really gone into the ethics of it," Wade said, shrugging.

They walked on in silence for a while. Wade glanced sidewise at the girl, seeing her in profile, young and fresh complexioned, with her expression maturely serious.

"It's all part of the technique of control," Wade said presently. "In times of crisis this kind of thing always happens. The truth is distorted, and steps are taken to keep the behaviour of the masses within predictable limits. But it's for their own good, and their overall chances of survival are better."

She was looking at him curiously, he noticed.

"Or don't you agree with me?" he added.

"I'm not quite sure what you mean," she said.

"I mean that this kind of mental and physical control of the population—propaganda and rationing—always emerges during a national crisis, like during the war, for instance. But it's a necessary thing for survival."

"Their survival or ours?"

"Well—since you differentiate—theirs. I take it *our* survival is assured."

She nodded.

"Well, the controls are for *their* benefit."

Again the elusive, enigmatic smile that hardly touched her lips. She said: "You haven't been around long, have you, Mr. Wade?"

"You mean I've got it all wrong?"

"Not exactly. You've got the words right but you haven't read between the lines as yet. There are wheels within wheels."

"Tell me about them," he suggested.

They had stopped outside a restaurant in Aldwych, and it was obvious to Wade that they had reached the end of their walk and talk. "Some other time, Mr. Wade," she said, smiling. "In any case, I'm not at all sure that I'm right, or that I ought to talk about it, right or wrong."

She made to move into the restaurant, but Wade said quickly: "Are you lunching here?"

"Yes."

"Mind if I join you, Miss Vance?"

She hesitated for an instant. "Not at all."

He followed her into the restaurant.

Strange, Wade thought, how normal the world seemed on the surface. The mechanics of life went on as before. Here, in the restaurant, for instance, businessmen and office workers ate their lunch and read the *National Express* over their coffee. Others talked among themselves and joked occasionally. There were no observable symptoms of tension or uneasiness, despite the ever-present threat of earthquakes and the lurid rumours that were undoubtedly circulating all over the country.

Wade and Miss Vance found a small corner table and sat facing each other across a small vase of narcissi in the subdued light from a hanging chandelier. There was a subtle sense of intimacy, as on the occasions when he had taken Shirley to lunch, but he felt too sober to be good company. For a while he began to regret having broken away from his old routine, but philosophically he cast off the feeling.

The waitresses were busy and the service was slow. He said: "About those wheels...?"

She smiled thoughtfully and studied her fingernails. "I see it like this, Mr. Wade. We work in a government department, at a high level of confidence. We see all the facts, but I've seen more than you because I've been around longer. After a time the facts seem to make a pattern. Nothing is actually stated, but the pattern emerges just the same."

"Could be," Wade murmured.

"Take the Arctic camps, for instance. They're being erected just as quickly as is humanly possible. By midsummer there should be accommodation for perhaps half a million people from the British Isles. The Americans and Canadians are expected to house about four million. In Antarctica there may be further accommodation for about a million. Russia claims three million, but that sounds too optimistic."

"So..."

"Those camps are permanent, Mr. Wade. They include factory sites, reactor heating and lighting, and immense plant for recovering water from the ice cap. They're built to last for a long time—perhaps several generations."

"I know that," said Wade. "It shows just how serious the authorities regard this water business."

"It shows more than that, Mr. Wade. Those camps are built for long-term survival in a world where there is no water."

"But we can't be absolutely certain there won't be any water. Engineers are working on pipelines and deep level bores..."

Again the enigmatic smile. "Even if they succeeded they couldn't produce more than a trickle. There are more than two billion people in the world. And my guess is that the main engineering effort is going into the construction of the polar camps. It's no easy job, Mr. Wade."

"I guess you're right," Wade admitted, feeling uncomfortably naïve in the girl's cool, intelligent gaze. "But the survival camps are only one half of the picture. The real struggle will be fought out here, in England and Europe and all the civilised countries of the world."

She shook her head. "There won't be any struggle."

"Meaning?"

"Before we came in here you were saying something about control of the population. You were right, Mr. Wade. The process of control is just starting. But it's not for *their* benefit—it's for *ours*. It's a ruthless rearguard action to keep the peace while the privileged ones pull out."

"Privileged ones?"

"You and I—the few chosen to survive."

Wade drummed his fingers on the table. "You're implying that about half a million people are going to be evacuated from this country to the Arctic, and the rest will be—abandoned."

"Something like that. There won't be any alternative. Once this emergency really gets under way civilisation will revert to the law of the jungle."

"You paint an ugly picture, Miss Vance. But it doesn't add up. If it were certain that only half a million people could survive, then there would have to be a fair and logical basis for selection. Why should I be chosen, anyway? What's so good about me?"

An ironic smile touched her lips. "Expedience, Mr. Wade. Logic plays little part in it. The survivors must have certain qualities that will facilitate the act of withdrawal. Sir Hubert Piercey evidently considered that you have certain essential qualities for the job you are doing. So you become one of the chosen—and just to make sure your motives stay pure, your family is taken out of danger. Naturally when the crisis breaks you will want to join them. There would be no question of your *not* wanting to be a survivor under those conditions, would there?"

"I suppose not."

"And I," she said quietly, "am one of the chosen too. You see, my father is an important executive on the permanent staff of the Exchequer."

Wade said nothing.

"So you are a lucky man, Mr. Wade. No relatives or friends in important government circles, and yet you are chosen to survive." A pause, followed by an inscrutable narrowing of the eyes. "Unless, of course, your wife…?"

Wade shook his head. "No important relatives whatever."

"Influential friends, perhaps?"

"No."

"Oh, well…"

Wade glanced around the room, looking for a waitress. They were all still busy, and the service was damned slow. It was their own fault for sitting in an obscure corner.

Miss Vance went on: "I suppose she was terribly shocked when you told her…"

Wade turned back to the girl. "You mean—going to the Arctic? No—I don't think she was shocked particularly. She seemed to take it in her stride."

"Perhaps she already knew?"

"How could she?"

The girl shrugged. "At all events, whatever the reason, you are one of the survivors."

And that, Wade thought afterwards, was a rather mysterious thing for anyone to say.

A moment later a waitress came to the table, and they ordered lunch.

Back in the office that afternoon Colonel Brindle came in to see him. "Busy time ahead for you, Wade," he announced without preamble, flinging a sheaf of official documents on to the desk. "Rationing starts at midnight tomorrow. There will be no official announcement until seven o'clock tomorrow evening—that's to avoid panic buying. I want you to prepare suitable material for radio and television announcements, and there will be a special evening edition of the *National Express* giving full details."

Wade stroked his chin thoughtfully. "Rationing of what?"

"Everything. Food, fuel, petrol, textiles—the lot."

"And water?"

"Not as yet—but reservoirs will arrange their own rationing system for the time being. We're recommending they should turn all water supplies off except for one hour in the mornings and a couple of hours in the evenings."

"That won't be popular," Wade said in a subdued voice. "Have the ration books been distributed?"

"They are waiting collection at post offices throughout the country. There will be a registration system. Later we'll set up official rationing centres."

Wade nodded without enthusiasm.

"You'll find all the information you need in those papers," Brindle said, pointing to the desk. "I'll vet the broadcast and press copy, and cyphered duplicates will have to be sent over the I.B.I. network. You might fix that with Patten."

"Okay," said Wade. Brindle hurried out of the office.

Slowly Wade picked up the papers and glanced through them. Foolscap pages bearing single-spaced typing, running on and on for twelve, thirteen, fourteen pages dealing with allocations, classifications, coupon values, variable points rationing, special categories for babies, expectant mothers, old age pensioners, tobacco restrictions, animal foodstuffs, hospital provisioning—and the legal penalties for infringement of regulations, and further penalties for wasting water, and a host of appendices outlining the more complex and obscure aspects of the situation.

Wade sighed and glanced at his wristwatch. Reading the document in itself was going to be an afternoon's work. Wearily he settled down in his chair and turned to page one.

VII

With the advent of rationing came the first signs of civil unrest. Teletyped reports from the big industrial towns brought curt details of demonstrations and political rallies accompanied in some cases by violence and bloodshed. Troops moved in overnight and armed patrols walked the streets. Then came the strikes—a quick series of industrial stoppages, undoubtedly Communist-inspired, culminating in a major engineering dispute involving twenty-two manufacturing concerns and nearly half a million workers in heavy industry. An incredible thing happened: fifteen of the firms went into voluntary liquidation, and the strike was over—indeed, all strikes were over.

The steel glove of military control began to tighten its grip. Rationing in itself was bad enough, but a new and even more terrifying threat was slowly revealed—the spectre of mass unemployment. The liquidation of the engineering firms, effective though it had been as a strike-breaking move, had, in fact, been occasioned through necessity. It started with the shipyards and associated industries; as the sea level dropped by thirty feet, creeping to forty and fifty and beyond, it became only too evident that the seas and oceans were no longer available for navigation. Ships were already obsolete, and there was no point whatever in continuing to make them.

The paralysis spread to other industries. The critical shortage of fuel oil and petrol, and the closing of export markets coupled with the complete cessation of imports, spread like leprosy throughout the factories of the country. The unemployed total grew steadily—two million, three million—then began to snowball. Ten million, twelve million, fifteen million... Rationing became meaningless. There was no work and consequently no money to buy even the rations that were available.

It happened quickly, in the course of three weeks, and so quickly that Wade found himself scarcely able to comprehend the enormity of what was taking place. For one thing he was out of it all, an objective observer building up an incredible picture from terse, impersonal signal messages, cushioned by privilege against the horrific reality of the unprivileged masses. He read the facts and computed the statistics, and continued to live his own life; as a government executive he could still use his car, drawing a restricted but adequate ration of petrol. Driving along the deserted roads of London got to be a harassing (and, indeed, embarrassing) ordeal, and it wasn't long before he ran into trouble. It started in a small way, with jeers from gangs of unemployed men loitering in the streets. Then came stones. One morning, driving from his home into the centre of London a brick crashed through his windscreen. He drove on defiantly past the angry gesticulating mob, forcing his mind to remain calm and dispassionate. You couldn't blame them, after all. The brick was merely a gesture of the universal resentment against the government, against the trend of events in general. It was an act of defiance against privileged officialdom. It was the subversive act of the desperate—the beginning, perhaps, of incipient chaotic anarchy.

Wade had underestimated the temper of the people. Three days later, driving along Bayswater Road, with not another car in sight, he found himself confronted by a group of some thirty men, strung out across the road. He debated for a moment, uncertain as to whether he ought to stop or crash right through them. He braked suddenly, and they closed in on him.

A thin-faced, wild-eyed man opened the offside door and said fiercely: "Government bastard—we'll show you." Wade slid along the seat away from him. The other door opened and a muscular arm hooked him round the neck. In an instant he was spread-eagled in the road and they were on him in a mass, punching and kicking and dragging him towards a side street. He caught a brief agonised glimpse of the car turned on its side and the air was full of the sound of splintering glass and the harsh crash of metal on metal. A moment later the concussion of an explosion roared in his ears, and later, before he lost consciousness, he saw the ugly, battered shape of his car spurting flames and belching smoke.

That was Wade's first experience of mob violence, but not his last. He learned in hospital that he had been rescued by a military patrol, and that two men had been shot dead during the act of rescue. The detective who interviewed him while he was still in bed wrapped in bandages assured him that, but for the intervention of the troops, he would certainly have been murdered. Such was the mood of the people.

Wade spent ten days in hospital recovering from general shock. Physically the damage was superficial, apart from an ugly laceration across his scalp. They had shaved off his hair, of course, and his enforced baldness both worried and amused him at the same time. His shaven head was adorned by a large area of white lint and plaster, like an Easter hat.

Patten came to see him in hospital, and also Brindle. They brought cigarettes and, secretively, a bottle of whisky and a bottle of brandy. Wade recognised that the gifts were indeed a luxury, for spirits, and even beer, were in short supply, and prices had rocketed to a fantastic level. The whisky, for instance, had cost more than seven pounds for the bottle, and the brandy nearer ten.

He had one other visitor, welcome and at the same time, because of his shaven head, unwelcome, and that was Miss Vance. She brought him a packet of cigarettes (fifteen shillings for twenty) and smiled at his grotesque appearance. She sat on a chair beside his bed and eyed him mischievously.

"You look cute," she observed.

"So do you," Wade countered.

"I'm glad it wasn't anything more serious, Mr. Wade. Things are getting bad."

Wade computed that he had already been in hospital five days. "What's happening?" he asked. "Outside, I mean."

"Oh—a kind of unofficial insurrection. It's to be expected I suppose. What with unemployment and rationing and the cost of living going up and up…"

"Is anything being done?"

"Well, yes—in a way. The government are issuing relief money on a large scale. They must be working overtime printing banknotes. The trouble is that the money loses its value overnight. You'd hardly recognise some of London's streets—they've got mobile field kitchens installed, with people queueing for miles, waiting for free meals. But there's a great deal of looting going on. Shops have emptied their windows, and troops are guarding the main shopping centres—particularly food shops."

"And the water situation…?"

She smiled grimly. "You haven't heard, of course. The oceans are draining away faster and faster. Professor Spendle has estimated that the Atlantic will be dry inside eight weeks, and the Pacific in about three months."

"There haven't been many earthquakes recently."

"Nothing phenomenal—just minor tremors. I think, perhaps, that the worst damage has been done."

Wade looked at her for a long time without speaking, trying to build up in his mind a picture of the overall situation. You had to accept the fact that a crisis of this type must inevitably produce a profound and violent reaction among the mass of the population. This was more than famine, and more than drought: it was, in a sense, a virulent plague, spreading swiftly throughout the world, depriving men of all they possessed, and taking away security. Naturally they would revert to a more fundamental level of behaviour. The niceties of civilised social conduct must go by the board. The basic survival drive must dominate every thought and act. Only rigid and uncompromising control by authority could maintain law and order, and then only for a limited period.

"Is anything being done on a scientific level?" he asked.

"You mean pipelines and bores?"

He nodded.

"Yes—I believe something is being done in a small way. But more important things are taking place on the psychological plane. Radio, television and the press. You're missing all the fun, Mr. Wade."

"Such as?"

"Song plugging, for one thing. The top hit number right now is a thing called 'Shoulder to Shoulder'—all about how we are all brothers and sisters in arms, facing whatever might come with cheerfulness and optimism. You can hear it twenty times a day or more."

"What else?"

She averted her eyes. "Pornography, I'm afraid—or something pretty near to it. In the papers and on television. You'd be surprised how the circulation of the *National Express* has grown during the last few days. And last night's television audience was estimated to be in the thirty million region."

"For what purpose?" Wade asked.

"A form of brainwashing—something to distract the mind of the average man from the horrors of everyday life…"

"And women?"

"Apparently the women don't matter. The men are the trouble-makers, and the whole propaganda machine is getting to work on the male sex."

"I see," said Wade. "I suppose a little pornography on the television screen keeps the men off the streets at night…"

"The men who are most likely to make a nuisance of themselves."

"And how is it all going to end?" Wade asked.

She shook her head doubtfully. "A gradual breaking down of civilisation, of lawful conduct. As I see it everything depends on the amount of charity the government can dispense. I don't think the brainwashing can be effective for long."

"And what about us?"

"I don't know, Mr. Wade. There is talk of establishing a kind of government residential zone between Kingsway and Whitehall, sealed off with barbed wire and machine guns. It may come to that yet."

He took her hand and squeezed it gently. "Thanks, Miss Vance," he said. "You've cheered me up no end. The future looks very rosy indeed."

She acknowledged his irony with a thin smile, and returned the pressure on her hand. Something electric seemed to surge momentarily through his veins.

She said: "People I know pretty well call me Susan, or even Sue."

Wade nodded. "I'll make a note of it."

"What do your friends call you?" she asked.

"All sorts of things. Sometimes they call me Philip, or even Phil."

"I'll make a note of it too," she murmured.

She left soon after, and Wade spent the next hour pondering the dark future, and occasionally thinking of Susan Vance, and the exhilarating sense of her presence, and in particular the excitement of the physical contact when he had touched her hand. Not once did he think of Janet.

When Wade was discharged from hospital and returned to his home, he found that the house had been ransacked. Everything of value, however trivial, had been stolen. The rear windows had been smashed and the greater part of the furniture was missing. They had taken his clothes, his books, his portable typewriter, and worst of all, they had taken the small stockpile of cigarettes and whisky that he had been carefully building up.

He inspected the desolate rooms, stripped of carpets and lino, and the bedrooms, stripped of beds and bedding, and cursed humanity as a whole. He attempted to phone the police, but found that the microphone unit had even been stolen from the handset.

From a callbox he notified the police, and presently they came round and investigated, but their manner was indifferent and lethargic. This sort of thing was going on all the time, the sergeant pointed out. Property no longer had any value. Crime had become a natural function of society. The world consisted of have-nots for the most part, and they took what they wanted from the haves. There was little the police could do about it. But they made notes and compiled an inventory of the stolen items, then said good morning and departed.

Wade returned to his office in the Consort Building. He travelled in a crowded Underground train. No buses were running, because of the fuel shortage, and the only remaining modes of transportation were the electric train services and a number of horse-drawn taxis.

Patten was in his office when he arrived—a frantic and bewildered Patten, partially engulfed in a small mountain of documents.

Patten breathed a huge sigh of relief when he saw Wade. He stretched out his arms and smiled broadly. "Wade," he said happily, "you're the nicest thing I've seen in days." He stood up and waved one arm in a gesture of renunciation over the desk. "It's all yours, Wade. I've had more than my fill."

As an afterthought he added: "Are you well?"

"Well enough," Wade conceded.

He settled down to work with no great enthusiasm. The signals from other I.B.I. centres overseas were depressing in the extreme. In Italy there had been wide-scale riots and the troops had killed more than twenty thousand people. China was a land of the dead, and the dead lay everywhere in the streets of the towns and in the open country. Japan had virtually ceased to exist. Martial law was the order of the day in Australia and New Zealand. Russia had embarked upon a programme of eugenic control of population, selecting those most suited for survival on a dialectical and ideological basis, and exterminating those who failed to reach the required standard. The United States of America was a land divided among itself, with individual states demanding and acquiring autonomy, and dealing with their own particular problems as they severally saw fit. But everywhere death was a prominent factor;

indeed, surveying the statistics as a whole, death had become a scientific and legitimate technique in the fight for survival. Death applied technically, perhaps politically, sometimes impartially, but always according to the rules.

Slowly Wade began to build up a picture of the world situation. During the ten days he had been in hospital there had been dramatic developments in the outside world. Sea level had fallen so rapidly that part of the bed of the Atlantic Ocean was already exposed, for the first time since the world began, to the light of day. Strange fish had been found in the oceanic mud and ooze—fish that had made headlines in the *National Express*—and (this was the major news story of the past week) the remains of the *Titanic* had been uncovered by the receding ocean. Rain had stopped abruptly, all over the world, it seemed. Although it was still early April, the sun had been shining warmly for more than a week from an unclouded sky, and shining with an unaccustomed intensity. The ground, in fields and allotments and gardens, was already cracking from dryness, and seedling plants were dying in their billions. Water was still unrationed, in the sense that no coupon system had yet been introduced, but the water boards and reservoir authorities were exercising stringent control. The early liberal allowance of three hours' water supply per day had been cut to two, and then to one, and a signal on Wade's desk announced a further cut to take effect at midnight: as from tomorrow water would only be available for thirty minutes each morning.

Food stocks, according to documentary evidence, were low. Worse still, the meteorological office predicted a hot dry summer with no rainfall at all, and it looked as if there would be no harvest worth mentioning. A secret international conference had taken place to ascertain the feasibility of international exchange of surplus foods during the early phase of the crisis, but no decision had been reached, partly because no country could envisage the possibility of having any surplus food stocks at all, and partly because exporting and importing would of necessity have to be effected by air, and the trickle of provisions so obtained would not materially alter the situation in any one continent.

These were the physical things, the basic commodities of life. But there were subtle changes too on the psychological level. The churches, for instance, were recording a considerable revitalisation of religious worship. In all countries people were entering the House of God in increasing numbers to pray for deliverance. Their gods were manifested in different forms, according to the nature of their faiths, but the basic motive was the same, whatever the colour or creed. Mankind, in the face of imminent peril, was seeking help from the supernormal.

One particular document aroused Wade's interest. It was an analysis of stock positions in the breweries and distilleries, and the outlook was not particularly bright. Production had ceased, of course: all water-consuming industries in the non-essential categories had long since ceased operation. Supplies of existing stocks were being released on a quota basis to the retail trade, but the quotas were so small that Wade realised at once that there must inevitably be a famine, or perhaps drought was the correct word, in alcoholic drinks. He was conscious of a distinct feeling of irritation. True, during his sojourn in hospital he had been virtually teetotal—the whisky and brandy that Brindle and Patten had brought him had hardly been touched due to the vigilance of the nurses—and he had seriously considered staying on the wagon, but this was different; it was one thing to break a habit by the exercise of sheer will-power in normal times, when whisky was available in almost every street of the city, but quite another thing to be forced into long-term sobriety by the simple non-availability of the medium of his vice. Even more galling was the recollection that thieves had taken ten bottles of very good Scotch from his home. He resolved to replace his stockpile at all costs.

At lunchtime he made a circuit of the public houses and off-licences, determined to order all the whisky he could reasonably afford, but nine out of every ten were closed, and the few that were open were selling only draught beer, and not more than one pint to each customer. The barmaid at the Globe in Fleet Street hinted at the reason for the absolute disappearance of spirits.

"It's the big hotels," she said. "They're paying sky-high prices. Twenty pounds a bottle for whisky and gin—building up stocks. My guvnor's already disposed of every bottle he had in the cellar. Wines, spirits, liqueurs, the lot—all gone to the big hotels on the Black Market. God knows what he thinks he's going to do with the money."

"Maybe he's going to buy himself a plot of ice at the North Pole," Wade suggested sardonically.

She stared at him, frowning. "Funny you should say that, Mr. Wade. There's been talk about something going on up there in the Arctic, like as if this water business is really serious, as if the only water left in the world is going to be ice."

Wade smiled with his lips, but not with his eyes. "You mustn't pay too much attention to rumours, Marie."

"I suppose not. I was reading in the *National Express* only this morning that they expect to have pipelines working by June. I dare say they're going to melt the ice and pump water down to all the reservoirs…"

"That seems very reasonable," Wade murmured.

"When that happens," Marie said, "the Black Market will come to a stop and I'll be only too glad to let you have a bottle of whisky, Mr. Wade."

He laughed briefly. "One bottle's no good, Marie. I want a hundred bottles."

She looked at him with open disbelief.

During the afternoon Colonel Brindle came into his office and made himself comfortable in a steel and plastic chair. He offered Wade a cigar, and Wade accepted the luxury, conscious of the fact that cigarettes and cigars were virtually extinct. Brindle's pale blue eyes looked rather dreamy, and his long jaw seemed sadder than ever.

He said: "Glad to see you fit again, Wade. The department needs your imaginative touch. Patten did his best but he knows his limitations, and so do we."

Wade said nothing—just moved his lips into a sour shape.

Brindle drew heavily on his cigar. He said: "For ten days you've been out of touch with events. You've probably noticed changes."

"Just a few," Wade conceded.

"You were unlucky. The mob who attacked you and destroyed your car are one of the toughest in London right now. The police have already attributed more than thirty murders to them. All the same, running a car is getting to be a risky business. It pays to keep to the major roads where the patrols are at hand."

"I was on a major road at the time."

"I know, Wade—but patrols have been quadrupled since then."

An interval of silence while they drew on their cigars. Blue grey smoke ascended lazily towards the white ceiling.

"I understand your home was burgled," Brindle said presently.

"I'm afraid so."

"Lose much?"

"Pretty well everything. In particular two thousand cigarettes and ten bottles of Scotch."

Brindle waved one hand nonchalantly. "You're better without them, but if you really need the stuff I can fix it."

"Well, thanks, Colonel. I guess I don't really need it, but I hate to be without it. But you didn't come here to talk about my morbid appetites."

Brindle grinned briefly. "No, I didn't. As a matter of fact I came to discuss certain immediate plans. The country is in an ugly mood. People don't understand clearly what is happening, but they are aware of the rationing and the restrictions, and they tend to be hostile towards government officials, as you ought to know."

Wade nodded.

"You're not the only one to suffer assault, Wade. Kennedy of the Statistical Department was beaten up three days ago. Brace from Accounts was slashed not twenty yards from his home. Even worse, Miss Graham from the Computing Division was attacked and raped by four thugs the day before yesterday. I had a call from the hospital about two hours ago. She's dead."

All Wade could say was: "I'm sorry." He didn't know the girl, but the horror reverberated in his mind for several minutes.

"In view of all this, the department has decided to take certain steps to safeguard members of the staff. We have requisitioned the Waldorf Hotel, just round the corner. It is to be residential quarters for the staff, where they will be within three minutes' walk of Consort Building. Naturally every facility will be available. We have taken steps to ensure that our people will be as comfortable as possible under the prevailing conditions."

Wade thought of his own derelict home and found himself very much in favour of the scheme. He said so.

"Good," Brindle commented. "You have no choice, anyway. This is an order, with no appeal. It is the first step towards the establishment of a barricaded governmental zone extending towards Charing Cross and beyond—to Whitehall. We're taking over other hotels too. The area is to be evacuated, apart from government staff, and we plan to build a helicopter port just off the Strand. We anticipate that road transport will become steadily more hazardous."

"I get the impression," Wade said, "that we seem to be preparing for some kind of siege—with a helicopter escape route available should the need arise."

Brindle nodded slowly. "It may come to that. We believe that we have everything under control—up to a point. But things are moving so quickly, and it is impossible to determine exactly how the mass of the population will react to further hardships. We are simply taking the obvious precautions."

"When do we move into the Waldorf?" Wade asked.

"Today, if you are ready. At all events, the sooner the better."

"I'm ready now," said Wade.

Brindle nodded appreciatively. "Sensible man. I'll get the Personnel Department to assign you to a room. Naturally, things may be a bit chaotic for a day or two, but we shall soon settle in."

Brindle stood up and walked towards the door. "I'll give you a buzz later. And incidentally, I'll fix you up with a crate of Scotch and a crate of gin."

"I'm not sure that I can afford it," Wade said.

"It's on the house," Brindle remarked, waving a hand generously. "Money isn't worth the paper it's printed on any more."

After Brindle had gone, Wade found himself sinking into a pensive mood. Suddenly, and unreasonably, the world seemed fantastic and dreamlike. Economics had gone haywire. Money had no value, but nevertheless the privileged ones could get what they wanted without money, could live in the Waldorf, could eat and drink and erect barricades to keep out the unprivileged and violent mob outside. It was a stark division of the world into two classes—the survivors and the non-survivors. An arbitrary distinction that could not be justified by any standards. And yet, when you were one of the potential survivors, standards didn't seem to matter any more. The mob was the mob—the brutal sadistic mob, killing and maiming and raping. You got to hate them for what they were, and, even worse, for what they would inevitably become as time went on.

But on the surface it wasn't too apparent. There were shortages and deprivations, and people grumbled and complained, but when you talked to them they were normal enough, and they shared a kind of petulant optimism. The violent factions were as yet a minority—a terrorist underground movement abhorred by the mass of the populace, but, Wade feared, gaining ground from day to day. Nevertheless life went on, and in certain respects it retained an everyday atmosphere. The cinemas, for instance, were still functioning, as were the theatres and revues, and the dance halls, and the night clubs. It was as if entertainment had acquired a priority value in governmental strategy.

You could walk down Kingsway, or the Strand, or any road or street for that matter, and see little that was unusual, apart from the absence of buses and the scarcity of cars. It was only when you looked a little closer that you began to detect the symptoms of social and industrial malaise: the empty offices and factories with the closed doors, the groups of idle men at street corners, the smashed windows of houses and shops that could have been due to earthquakes or malicious intent, the queues outside the official relief centres and the field kitchens.

Wade was reminded vaguely of the depression of the early thirties, and in many ways the situation was parallel. Unemployment, a shortage of essential commodities, universal flagging of the racial spirit—and the same underlying sense of resentment and bitterness, expressed in a subdued way, modified and disciplined to some extent by the calculated propaganda of the public information channels.

Walking down Kingsway towards Aldwych and the Waldorf Hotel, Wade looked around at the tall stately buildings of London. They seemed ageless—timeless—almost a geometrical configuration of the underlying bedrock itself. Then he looked at the people around him, crowding the pavements as they walked towards the nearest tube station; ordinary people, with their own secret hopes and fears and loves and hates, each an individual, yet each also a part of the mass. He realised suddenly that there was no threat from the individual—the threat came from the mass of individuals acting in unison under the pressure of hysteria; and yet each act of violence, when it came, would be the act of an individual, but an individual sinking his identity in the blind psychological organism of the mob, reacting and behaving as a limb of that superior mass organism. Individuals—but each one a mob in himself.

Musing on the self-contradictions of the concept, he entered the elegant foyer of the Waldorf and was welcomed by the uniformed porter.

*

Wade settled in Room 624. It was a large cream-washed room with a wide window overlooking the Aldwych and facing the immense grey stone fascia of Bush House. There was a single bed with a resilient mattress, a small table, two or three chairs, a pendant lamp with a wide saucerlike shade and an ornate fireplace blocked and fitted with a two-bar electric fire.

Colonel Brindle was better than his word: three days after moving into the Waldorf four crates were delivered to Wade's room. He checked over the contents with the casual air of a connoisseur. Brindle had evidently pulled a few wires, for the crates contained the equivalent of a respectable cocktail bar—in addition to whisky and gin there was an assortment of fortified wines and liqueurs, and even a bottle of vodka. He smiled in grim appreciation as he checked the bottles and replaced them in the crates. Now that they were here, he found that he didn't particularly want any of them. The craving of the early days in the hospital had evaporated, and an inner stubbornness had taken possession of him.

Brindle had also sent cigarettes—about two dozen boxes of a hundred—but he pushed those to one side also. He hadn't smoked in ten days and was just a little proud of his self-discipline.

Later in the evening, however, he relented. He sampled the whisky and smoked two cigarettes, then took a little more whisky, then (purely out of curiosity, he told himself) tried the vodka. Then back to the whisky. That night he slept soundly and dreamlessly. But it was only a lapse. During the next few days he resumed his new-found abstinence, and felt the better for it—spiritually, if not physically.

On his fifth day in the Waldorf he received a letter from Janet. The envelope was official and unstamped, bearing a printed insignia and the words: *Essential Government Mail.* The postmark was smudged and indistinct, but appeared to read: *Zone 4—Sector B.*

The letter was written on thin paper (air mail, obviously) in Janet's back-sloping feminine hand. It was not a long letter, nor was it very informative, but the contents were reassuring.

We are comfortably installed, she had written. *This is a cold bleak wilderness, with temperatures about forty below, and gales reaching sixty miles an hour. But the huts are warm enough, and there is plenty of food and warm clothing. David likes it here. He is going to school with other boys, and has plenty of friends. There are five other women in my hut, and between us we have quite a good time. But we miss our men, which means, Phil, that I miss you. We get news by a wired radio system, but we don't know how true it is. I understand we can now write to each other, so please tell me everything that is going on in London.*

The letter continued in more personal and intimate terms, but on the whole it was inconclusive and, characteristically for Janet, lacking in essential detail. He gained a vague picture of some kind of communal life, rather on barrack lines—a picture of ordinary people adapting themselves to everyday routine in an incredible environment and in the end taking it for granted. The fact that David was at school (but what kind of school?) indicated that authority was taking a long-term view of the Arctic settlement. He felt pleased that Janet had feminine company—that would tend to neutralise any feeling of loneliness, if, indeed, it existed at all.

Dimly and insidiously at the back of his mind an idea was germinating from a poisonous seed that had been implanted by a casual word from Miss Vance. *Influential friends, perhaps? At all events, whatever the reason, you are one of the survivors.* Innocent words, taken out of context, and innocent enough taken in context. Perhaps too innocent.

I must think about it some time, he told himself. If Miss Vance knows anything, she will tell me sooner or later. I'll make her tell me. Meanwhile, I'll write to Janet—a long letter, a nice letter, to make her happy. And David too, I'll write to him.

But he would have to talk with Miss Vance very soon, talk to her quietly and confidentially, cross-examining her about the unspoken implication of her words. And, somehow, it was comforting to reflect that Miss Vance's room in the Waldorf was 508, on the floor below—almost within shouting distance.

He resisted the impulse to pour himself a drink and, holding Janet's letter in his hand, thought about Miss Vance in her room just one storey below his.

VIII

UNTIL HIS HAIR HAD GROWN TO A RESPECTABLE LENGTH, Wade led a solitary life, avoiding his colleagues as much as possible both on and off duty. He criticised himself for his vanity, but had to admit that there was nothing he could do about it. The fact was that he was sensitive about his appearance, and he recognised that his urge to withdraw from contact with others was in the nature of a compulsion.

It was six weeks before all trace of baldness had been eradicated, and the new growth of hair pleased him. It was short and vigorous, cropped in an American style, and made him look younger. He celebrated with the aid of the whisky bottle and decided to call on Shirley Sye.

It was not a spontaneous decision, but rather the result of long premeditation during the weeks of self-imposed solitude. Wade was a changed man in several ways. For one thing he had learned the art of self-control to such an extent that smoking and drinking had ceased to be habitual. The addiction was destroyed, and he smoked and drank occasionally, by design, as an act of defiance. And it was in the same spirit of inverted stubbornness that he made up his mind to visit Shirley Sye.

Nor was there any confusion in his motives. He was a lonely individual, but loneliness was an integral part of his nature and he accepted it as such; it was a negative background from which he could make a positive action. Just as he could now, if he wished, force himself to drink half a bottle of whisky after a week of sobriety, so also he could reach out for Shirley, breaking the normal pattern of his behaviour in a bout of emotional intoxication. Thus he argued with himself, rationalising the urge that had been building up inside him for so long, and knowing all the time that he needed Shirley because she was a woman, and even more important, because she would be available at short notice.

He made up a parcel containing a bottle of gin, a bottle of vermouth and a hundred cigarettes, and as a concession to himself included a half bottle of whisky. If Shirley was one of the have-nots (and there was no reason to suppose otherwise) she would welcome the gift—and the giver. He tied the parcel securely with string and left the hotel.

The Underground trains were few and far between these days, in an effort to conserve power; consequently they were always crowded. He had to stand all the way to Maida Vale, and was relieved when he was able to get out into the open air again. People were looking weary and hollow-eyed, and not a little shabby (understandable, of course, in view of the situation), and to have them about him, pressing against him, in the gaunt atmosphere of the train, made him feel uneasy.

Several loafers at a street corner eyed him curiously as he walked towards Lawrence Avenue. His sense of uneasiness increased, but he tightened his grip on the parcel and lengthened his stride. Glancing back quickly as he reached the corner of the avenue he saw that they were following him—a pack of five lean, sullen men moving with slow shambling steps.

He turned the corner, resisting an impulse to run, and hurried to Shirley's address. This was a tree-lined road of terraced houses, faded and crumbling here and there, which had been divided into flats. Shirley lived in the upper apartment at number seventeen. He pressed the appropriate bell-push and waited.

The pack had arrived at the corner of Lawrence Avenue. He could see them reflected in the bay window of the house; they were standing idly and silently, just watching.

It may be, he thought, that Shirley has gone away. She may even be dead for all I know. I should have kept in touch during the past months. He rang the bell again and almost immediately the door swung open.

It was Shirley—the same poised Shirley with her sleek black hair and hazel eyes, with the same sallow complexion, and yet not quite the same Shirley, for there was something about her appearance, a certain carelessness, that seemed out of key.

No surprised reaction—no sudden welcoming smile—just a slight quizzical raising of the eyebrows and a subtle change of expression that might have been suspicion.

"Hello, Shirley," Wade said.

"Hello, Phil. It's been a long time."

He nodded.

"Won't you come in?"

He followed her into the hall and up the stairs to her flat. The room was small and overcrowded with furniture. A hide-covered armchair jostled an old-fashioned couch in the window bay. The centre of the floor was occupied by a heavy oak table, matching the old-fashioned sideboard against one wall. The wallpaper was green, with a pattern of slender leaves and flowers. On the floor was brown lino, covered in part by a threadbare carpet. Two chairs stood idly in front of the empty grate.

Shirley turned to face him. The light reflecting from the green wallpaper made her look sallower than ever, Wade thought. She was old—older than the desirable image stored in his memory.

Her grey skirt was creased and the white blouse she was wearing was soiled around the neckline.

She noted the movement of his eyes. "I've changed, haven't I, Phil?" she said.

"We've all changed," Wade remarked, placing the parcel on the table. He took her arms and said, with more enthusiasm: "But it's good to see you again, Shirley. How have you been making out?"

She withdrew from him. "Like everyone else, I haven't." She indicated the armchair. "Won't you sit down?"

Wade sat on the couch, wondering if she would join him, but she remained standing, looking at him without expression.

"I'm afraid I can't offer you anything," she said. "I do have a little coffee but there's no water to spare and no gas to heat it with anyway."

"That's all right," said Wade. "The days of hospitality are over—I know that. But the wish is there, and that's the thing that matters."

She sat down wearily on one of the upright chairs. "You didn't come here to talk platitudes."

"No—I came, well—for old time's sake. To see you and talk a little…"

"Nice of you," she murmured without conviction. "Are you still in this government job…?"

"Yes."

"So you're doing all right, I suppose."

"Well—it depends how you look at it. In a sense I guess you'd say we are privileged. We just work and obey orders, and the powers that be keep us alive. It's that kind of a deal."

"It sounds a very nice kind of deal. It's a pity we can't all work for the government."

Wade shrugged, not happy at the trend of the conversation. "That's partly why I came here, Shirley—to find out how tough things are with you, and whether I can help."

"Are you taking a short- or long-term view?"

Wade did not understand what she meant, and said so.

"Well, let's face it, Phil—what good can help, as you call it, do? Prolong the agony a little longer, perhaps. We both know what the future holds."

"Do we?" Wade asked sceptically. "I wouldn't be too sure of that, Shirley. There's a great deal going on. Take the Messiter pipelines, for instance, pumping water from what's left of the Atlantic at the rate of ten thousand gallons an hour. And there are other projects under way."

"Ten thousand gallons an hour isn't much to an island of more than fifty million people. The trouble is, Phil, that your news is the official stuff—pipelines and so on. Perhaps you're out of touch with the real news—the stuff that doesn't qualify for the I.B.I. network."

"Such as..."

"The fact that there hasn't been any water in this district for nearly six days. Don't look surprised, Phil. We know all about the allocation system—thirty minutes of mains water at nine o'clock each morning. It's fine in theory, but it isn't allowed to work out in practice. The Black Market racketeers have moved in."

"How?" asked Wade, perplexed.

"By sabotaging the underground water main—not only here, but in other districts and other towns. Then what do they do? Simple. They go round in a truck selling water at five shillings a gallon. There's no alternative. We have to buy."

"But—can't the police do anything?"

"It's not illegal to sell water, and there's nothing to connect the sellers with the saboteurs. The water men say they are performing a public service, and the high charge is to cover costs—particularly Black Market petrol. The truth is that the police have more important things to worry about. It's not safe to walk along the street any longer. Violence and crime seem to be breaking out everywhere. People are being murdered for their clothing—even their shoes."

"I know about the gangs," Wade said thoughtfully. "I got beaten up myself."

"Then you probably know about the protection rackets. We've got ration books, yes—and the basic ration is supposed to be adequate, if austere. That's if it's honoured. The fact is you can't get the supplies for which you have coupons, because the shopkeepers have been forced to sell their stocks to Black Market gangs, or risk having their premises set afire—or even worse. Only last week, Mr. Maple, the grocer, was beaten up for not co-operating, and his wife was kidnapped and raped and left for dead on the Watford road. But you're an I.B.I. man—you ought to know about these things."

Wade shook his head slowly. "I'm afraid the information which passes through my department isn't so detailed. It's more on an international level—the broad picture of world events."

"Then you ought to get down to local detail once in a while," Shirley said bitterly. "How do you suppose people like me can exist? I live off the Black Market but for that I need money. A loaf of bread off the ration costs eight shillings or more. It can cost as much as twenty pounds to survive for one week. And things will get worse."

Wade said nothing, just watching her uncomfortably. There was no great animation in her expression or tone of voice; she was merely reciting fact, familiar fact that called for no emotion other than resentment. He was beginning to realise that his evening out had been nothing more than a selfish pipe-dream.

"After the Stenniger group closed down I managed to get a job with an industrial firm in the electronics field—invoice typing. It lasted for six weeks, and then the firm quit business. I got another job, for three weeks as a shop assistant until the firm sold out. Since then I've been living on government relief—that's what they call it, anyway. I've used up all my savings—a hundred and sixty pounds of it—and I've sold everything that wasn't an essential—radio, television, typewriter, rings, jewellery—such as it was. There's nothing left to sell except myself, and women are a cheap enough commodity these days. You can have one for a packet of biscuits or half a pound of sugar."

A long pause while she regarded him bleakly. Then she continued: "Can I interest you, Phil, in a transaction of that kind? I've interested other men, and my terms are modest—indeed, generous."

Wade acknowledged the acidity of her voice and wished he had had the good sense to stay at the Waldorf.

She glanced at the brown-paper parcel on the table, then back at him. "I take it that's why you came here. A little help and help yourself. Only I'm curious about what you brought in the parcel. It's big, by present-day standards—too big for what I've got to offer."

"Shirley," said Wade, "you've got things all wrong. Sure, you're bitter, and you have a right to be. I can help and I will help. It's just that—well, I didn't think that things were quite so bad."

She stood up and crossed to the table, putting a hand on the parcel. "Can I open it, Phil?"

He came over to her, placing one hand on her arm. "I don't think I'd want you to, Shirley. Not now."

"But you brought it for me, didn't you?"

"In a way." He struggled to crystallise his confused thoughts. "I saw things differently. If I'd known what I know now I'd have brought a different kind of parcel."

She began to slip the string from the paper, and he could only watch her helplessly, unable to predict her reactions. She removed the wrapping slowly, almost leisurely, and uncovered the bottles. One by one she picked them up and stood them on the table—the gin, the vermouth and the whisky. She stood looking at them for what seemed to Wade a brief eternity, then, unhurriedly, she turned to him and swung her arm. It must have been one of the hardest slaps of all time: it rocked him back on his heels and half paralysed his cheek.

"I'm sorry, Shirley," Wade said. "I told you—I didn't realise how things were. I thought we could have a drink to celebrate…"

"Celebrate *what*?" There was plenty of animation in her now, he observed. Her face was pale and her lips taut.

"I won't even try to explain," he said resignedly. "But think it over. Tomorrow you may understand my point of view."

"I understand it *now*, Phil. You got a thing about me all of a sudden. Maybe it was a rebound from that other night a long time ago, when you turned me down—remember? You thought you could come here with the nectar—twenty quid a bottle if you can get it—and you thought maybe we could get high and loving and I'd be so grateful I'd give you the key to my flat. Well, you figured it all wrong. I'm not an enthusiastic amateur any more. I'm strictly professional and I'm building up a clientele, like most other women I know. If you want me you have to buy me, not seduce me. My price is cheap—dirt cheap."

She glanced again at the brown paper, moved it, and saw the boxes of cigarettes. She picked one up and eyed it speculatively.

"You overplayed your hand, Phil. For the cigarettes alone I'd have done business. They fetch a nice price these days. Me—I stopped smoking a long time back."

"I didn't come here to do business," Wade said angrily.

She smiled, but it was a cold smile. "Not my kind of business. You're living in the past, Phil. The niceties of social relationships are as dead as a dodo. Seduction is as old-fashioned as a chastity girdle—except perhaps among the privileged government employees. Remember I once told you—the general adaptation syndrome. The hardening of the individual in times of crisis—the desensitising of the spirit—the reversion to a more fundamental pattern of behaviour."

"I remember," Wade said.

"Well, then...?" She smiled again, but this time it was a calculated smile of affability. Slowly she replaced the cigarettes on the table.

"Perhaps I was hard on you, Phil. You came here for dirty motives, but you're no worse than most men. I'll forgive you, and what's more—for the cigarettes I'll do a deal. That makes it honourable by my standards."

"They weren't always your standards," Wade pointed out.

"Times have changed, Phil. The survival drive, remember?"

Wade made up his mind. "Shirley," he said, "I'm sorry I came—I really am. I guess I gave way to a sentimental mood..."

"Is *that* what you call it?"

"No matter. At least we understand each other. It was nice

seeing you again, and I'll help you as I promised. I can get food and money—plenty of money…"

"All for free?"

He nodded. "Yeah—all for free. As a guy with dirty motives it's the least I can do."

"I'm sorry I said that, Phil. I admit I was angry, but…"

"But you don't want to kill the goose that might lay golden eggs."

She came closer to him and took his arm. "Don't let's quarrel again, Phil. We used to be good friends. We can pick up where we left off. Stay with me tonight. We'll celebrate, like you said."

"We'll get high and loving," Wade suggested sardonically. She frowned at the echo of her words.

"You *are* angry, aren't you, Phil?"

He eyed her remotely. "No, Shirley, I'm not angry. I'm just plain cold sober, and seeing both of us as we really are. The trouble is, I don't like what I see. You were right—dead right. I came here to get what I could. I figured you'd be happy with the drink and I figured on setting myself up with a convenient bed partner. That's the kind of guy I am—methodical in the rottenest way. I didn't think of you at all, and I didn't attempt to look at things from your point of view."

"Why should you?" she demanded. "The world is coming to an end and we all have to think of ourselves."

"Is that part of the general adaptation syndrome, too?"

"Yes, Phil, it is. Now let's stop arguing. I'll get a couple of glasses."

"No," Wade said firmly. "You're being shrewd. You aim to be nice for what you can get out of me."

"It's a legitimate motive, Phil, and no worse than yours. Can't we laugh it off?"

"I'll try—tomorrow."

He walked towards the door, turning his back on her. As he reached it and turned the handle something moved swiftly over his shoulder. Glass shattered against the wall and liquid splashed over him. The air was full of the sweet, pungent smell of gin. He turned quickly. She was in a half crouched attitude, arms held stiffly before her, eyes ablaze with fury.

"You swine," she hissed. "Take the lot with you." Her hand reached out for the bottle of vermouth. Quickly he left the room, and as he closed the door the vermouth bottle smashed against it. Hurrying down the stairs he heard the crash of the whisky bottle, and after that her loud mocking laughter. It resonated in his ears until he reached the street.

Caution asserted itself. The road was clear of louts, but he was not prepared to take chances. Clenching his fists he advanced warily towards the road leading towards the tube station. The road was quiet enough, but four or five blocks down there was a throng of people grouped at a corner—both men and women. He decided to play safe, and crossed over the road, taking a side street to a parallel road that would lead towards Maida Vale tube station.

His progress was uneventful, but his mind was twisted in a mood of self-contempt. The resentment within him was directed against himself, not Shirley. She had spoken honestly enough and exposed his own shallowness—or was it shallowness? What was so shallow in supposing that Shirley was fundamentally the same woman as she had been months before? And how could any man reasonably predict the change that had taken place in her? Sure, he had been an opportunist, but these were opportunist days, and opportunism wasn't illegal if it came to the point.

She was hysterical, he told himself. Anyone might be hysterical living under these conditions. She had her emotional outburst and then it was all over. Hell, I could have stayed—she wanted me to in the end. I walked out like a spoiled child—no wonder she got mad.

I could go back—even now. Maybe it would be better that way. We could make up, and there's always fun in making up. Maybe we could get round to being adult instead of infantile. After a few drinks…

And then he remembered the smashing of the three bottles and the harsh taunting laughter.

He found himself approaching a church, and the air trembled with the remote sound of voices singing a hymn. He hesitated at the porch, then went in.

The church was filled to capacity, and people were standing in overflow at the rear near to the font. He joined them, remaining silent as the hymn continued, until the voices ceased and the organ rumbled into silence.

He had an irresistible urge to smoke and felt in his pocket for cigarettes, but stopped abruptly, remembering where he was. A voice came from across the congregation, a clear resonant voice, speaking with a veiled savageness. He missed the first few sentences, and his attention focused abruptly on a reference to hydrogen bombs.

"It must have been apparent to all men of Christian reason that in these hydrogen weapons was the nucleus of the ultimate evil," pronounced the minister. "They were designed for one specific purpose—destruction. They were tested to make sure that their capacity to destroy could not be bettered. The tests, they told us, were innocent and harmless. There could be no danger either to the present generation of humanity or to future generations.

"But God in his wisdom decided to challenge the lies told in the name of science. He decided to demonstrate once and for all the fallacy of what is known as scientific logic. He showed us the true power of the elemental forces with which scientists were experimenting—the power to destroy the world.

"We are seeing the world destroyed, slowly and inevitably, at the whim of the scientists and politicians. It is the supreme lesson which God in his mercy has seen fit to teach us. The ultimate power, the power that energises the living universe, does not stem from the laboratory or the atomic reactor or the nuclear weapon proving zone; it comes from the Divine Spirit that animates mankind and the world we live in.

"The lesson is being taught, and it is for us to learn the lesson. The forces of material science have been discredited for all time, and we must turn to God for our salvation…"

Wade left the church and made his way to the Underground. No comment, he said to himself. No comment at all. The scientists are certainly in an indefensible position. It all started with an H-bomb. Operation Nutcracker, and everything that came after. You can't blame the clergy for seeking a technological scapegoat—the preachers and the scientists have been at each others' throats for more than a century. But why drag God into it? God in his wisdom and God in his mercy. This is man's doing, the whole lousy business, and man has to face up to it, honourably or dishonourably, but at least with dignity, and without having to call on the supernatural for succour.

Let's face the facts, he thought. The world is finished. At any rate, it will be a very different world from the one which died when the last of the H-bombs was exploded in the South Pacific.

And the reason? No water. The tide has gone out—perhaps for ever. What difference does that make in the cosmic sense? What is nature's point of view? Evolution came slowly to a halt when the first primeval man lit a fire and made a wheel. Since then man has steadily ceased adapting himself to his environment, but has, on the contrary, adapted his environment to suit his own needs.

Suddenly the environment changes, but man has learned how to adapt it, if not himself. The waters of the world are draining away, but there is unlimited water locked away in the deep ice of the polar caps. And there is the solution, and there man in his ingenuity can find his salvation. The human race must necessarily be decimated, that is inevitable, and it is something that God in all his wisdom cannot prevent. Or in all his mercy.

And when the final hours come, Wade thought, when the dead are rotting in the sun-baked streets and the only water is that locked in the inanimate protoplasm, will the men of God still be using science as a whipping boy and urging us to learn the supreme lesson? What we are going to need, all of us, is not a lesson in religion or abstract ethics, but water pure and simple—H_2O—a simple combination of hydrogen and oxygen in specific relationship. And though we may pray to God, or whatever we believe in, it is the scientists who will eventually provide the solution. Those who have the power to destroy also have the power to create.

What the hell! he exclaimed mentally. I'm getting morbid in my old age, and a damned sight too metaphysical. What a night—a neurotic woman, a generous helping of sexual frustration, some forty pounds' worth of smashed liquor and a God's-eye view of the international crisis by an eloquent preacher—not forgetting the sullen, lean-faced men standing in silent groups on the street corners, waiting intently for potential victims.

He was glad when he reached the Underground station. The crowded train that had seemed so repugnant a little earlier was now a haven of safety. And Kingsway, when he reached it, was in a different world altogether. Here was security, for himself, and for what would eventually survive of the British portion of the human race.

It was nine o'clock when he entered the foyer of the Waldorf. He ascended in the elevator to the sixth floor and turned the key in the door to his room, then, on an impulse, stopped. Slowly he replaced the key in his pocket and walked down the stairs to the fifth storey. At room 508 he hesitated, uncertain of himself, but in the end he pressed the bell push.

A minute ticked by silently. She must be in, he thought. She doesn't normally go out. Where could she go, anyway? He pressed the bell push again.

At the third attempt it became obvious that Susan Vance was definitely not at home. Wade returned to his own room. He looked over the crates of drink and selected a fresh bottle of whisky.

"You've earned it, brother," he said to himself. "It's been that kind of a day."

He found a glass and poured himself a large measure of whisky, diluting it with a little water, and finished it within thirty seconds. Then he poured another.

He took the glass to the table, produced some paper and an envelope, and wrote a letter to Janet.

IX

CAME JUNE, AND THE HOT WEATHER PERSISTED, AND THE sky over Britain remained an intense, unclouded blue. The Atlantic and Pacific oceans became mud flats, rapidly drying out and cracking into vast jig-saw patterns, with their own fantastic vegetation of dying undersea flora. Billions of fish were destroyed as the waters receded, and among them were new sub-oceanic species that had never before been seen by man. In the oceans there were lakes of salt water left in declivities and hollows, but slowly they were giving up their water to the heat of the sun. The rivers of Britain had become rivulets trickling over baked river beds. The Thames was a shallow stream of sluggish water, and you could walk across it well into the estuary.

Full water rationing came into effect early in the month. All main supplies were cut off at the reservoirs, and bowser trucks delivered bulk allocations to improvised rationing centres in key districts. The basic ration was two gallons per person per day, but there was a special allowance for such industries as were still functioning. There were also stringent cuts in food rations. A new synthetic food consisting of a derivative of polythene foam plastic had been introduced: it was in effect a substitute for bread, and it provided bulk plus vitamins and glucose (and bromides, the cynics suggested).

Civil unrest and crime increased. There was an upsurge of racketeering and violence and murder, culminating in gang warfare in half a dozen of the principal cities of the British Isles. In America things were even worse, and the greater part of Europe was an anarchy rigorously and ruthlessly controlled by martial law. The English Channel was virtually dry, and there were fears that desperate Europeans would attempt to cross it in an effort to migrate north towards the Arctic ice.

The *National Express*, however, ignored the tragedy that was reported with every teletype message, and concentrated on what could only be described as the gimmicks of the situation. Long, illustrated features on the Messiter pipeline network; excited articles on the discovery of new water wells in rural areas; learned observations on scientific findings in the dry ocean beds; a big story proving that there never had been an Atlantis—and even religious articles interpreting the crisis in terms of character determination, which, Wade thought, was the cruellest cut of all.

He wrote many letters to Janet and David, and saw a great deal of Susan Vance. At first she had been vaguely hostile, because, she explained, for the six weeks following his stay in hospital he had seized every opportunity of avoiding her.

"It was deliberate," Wade explained. "I didn't like the look of my shaven head."

"I don't remember raising objections," Susan said.

"Nevertheless, I was being considerate in not inflicting my curious appearance on others."

"Am I others?" she asked, smiling.

"A very special kind of other, I guess."

"I'll forgive you," she said.

They were talking together over lunch at the Waldorf, where the ballroom had been converted into a restaurant for personnel from Consort Building. The food was austere enough, and had been deteriorating over the weeks, but it was still a banquet by external standards, and because of that Wade was never able to stifle a sense of guilt as he ate and drank. On this particular day the main dish was a composite of a kind of seasoned omelette (hens were still laying eggs, apparently, and feeding on stocks of dried corn stored from pre-crisis days) and reconstituted dehydrated potatoes. There were no green vegetables, for the agricultural land was arid and rapidly becoming barren, but spaghetti made an acceptable, if tasteless, substitute.

"It would be nice," Susan said, "to sample fish once in a while."

"You are talking of an extinct species," Wade commented.

"Funny when you think of it," she remarked. "All life came from the sea, according to the theory of evolution. And now the fishes are gone, perhaps for ever..."

"I suppose some of them will survive in the sub-oceanic cavities—in eternal darkness. They'll probably evolve into something quite different."

"In about ten million years. They may even inherit the earth."

"Not while there's ice at the poles."

Susan hesitated, then said: "I don't care to think about it, somehow. These last few weeks I've stopped looking into the future. I just take the present as it comes."

"So long as it keeps coming there's nothing to worry about," Wade remarked sardonically.

"Sometimes I wonder whether the most sensible thing to do isn't to get drunk, day and night, until the end."

"What end? I thought we were one of the survival group."

"We are in theory, Phil—but incredible things are happening and none of us can predict the course of events."

Wade shrugged. "Well, if you want to get drunk, I've got the wherewithals. We can get drunk together."

She raised her eyebrows questioningly.

"I have a private stock," he explained. "The result of a little internal wire-pulling. Candidly, I hardly touch it these days, but if you'd care to join me in a private cocktail party for two…"

She eyed him intently, in a way that made him feel slightly uncomfortable, but in a moment she smiled. "I think it's a wonderful idea, Phil."

"Tonight, perhaps?"

She nodded briskly. "Tonight."

And in such a way did Susan Vance become an integral part of Wade's complex emotional life.

Two days later there was a tremendous earthquake—the most devastating to date. The shock wave created havoc throughout the south-eastern area of England, tearing gigantic rifts in the ground, and shattering buildings on a wide scale in a score of major towns and cities. Oxford Street in London resembled the aftermath of an air raid, and the line of devastation spread well into the East End, destroying offices and shops and houses to Dagenham and beyond. The Waldorf Hotel danced in a crazy infernal jig for nearly half an hour, but it remained intact, apart from splintered windows. Immediately facing, a segment of Bush House crumbled, and an outside wall collapsed revealing stacked offices gaping hollowly above Aldwych.

Although the earthquake in itself was catastrophe enough, the after-effects were even worse. Fractures in the rock strata beneath London wrought havoc with underground structures, the tube railway system, the drains, water mains, gas pipes, electricity and telephone conduits. Communications were paralysed, and gas and electrical services were completely disrupted over a wide area. The signals that came into Wade's office made depressing, and sometimes horrific reading. Fires that had broken out had proved to be almost uncontrollable due to the critical shortage of water, and one particularly severe fire in the Poplar district had only been kept in check by dynamiting a large residential zone.

Although Wade did not realise it at the time, this was the beginning of the end. For one thing the weather was extremely hot, with temperatures rising above ninety Fahrenheit every day, and rain was a curious phenomenon of days long dead. Water had a rarity value, and one of the big problems that had arisen during recent weeks was that of sanitation: there was only an infinitesimal quantity of water available for the purpose of sanitary drainage. The sewage farms were derelict, and lavatory cisterns had become completely inoperative. Beneath every town and city was a network of pipes congested with drying sewage, and the earthquake burst them asunder.

Nothing happened for one week—two weeks—and then the first cases were reported over the communications network. Typhoid—five, seventeen, twenty-six, forty-nine, eighty-two, and on and on into the hundreds and thousands. And then, as the typhoid epidemic consolidated its grip on the population of south-east England, came the first hint of something even more terrifying. It was cholera.

The plague spread rapidly from its point of origin in Stepney, and the figures mounted rapidly. The hospitals, already overloaded with typhoid cases, were unable to cope with the new epidemic. Schools and church halls were taken over as emergency wards, and, as the death roll mounted, special furnaces were built to incinerate the victims of the plague.

To inhibit the spread of infection the government introduced special measures to prevent the migration of population from the affected Home Counties. All rail services were suspended, and road blocks, manned by troops, were erected on all roads to the north. And then, when armed gangs attempted to break through the barriers in a violent bid to escape from plague-ridden London, martial law was imposed. The first firing squads went into action.

Wade, along with the rest of the staff at Consort Building, underwent daily medical examinations and received countless hypodermic injections. Kingsway was sealed off with a stout barbed-wire fence patrolled by the military. The Underground railway system came to a halt, as did all traffic. The city settled down to a quiet and bitter paralysis.

From incoming reports he learned that London was by no means unique. Cholera had, of course, already wrought havoc in the Far East, and was even now springing up in most of the countries of Europe, and in Africa and South America. The United States and Canada, curiously enough, were free from plague so far, but there had been severe epidemics of typhoid. Inevitably all air transit between the continents of the world had come to a stop: it was as if all the authorities of the world had recognised that the threat of virulent disease was, for the moment, more important than the danger of thirst and starvation.

For Wade, confined to the Consort Building during the day and the Waldorf Hotel at night, life seemed to have little point. He was aware of a subtle impression of having been buried alive; the Kingsway zone was a tiny fertile oasis in a vast poisonous area of insidious death. The statistics, as they came from the Cypher Office, only served to increase his sense of desolation. Thirty thousand had died from cholera the previous day, and nearly two thousand from typhoid. Despite the abolition of all road and rail traffic the plague had spread northwards, and the first cases of cholera were being reported in Liverpool and Manchester, and as far away as Carlisle.

His only consolation, if such it was, lay in his maturing relationship with Susan Vance. Maturing because there was, between them, a certain indefinable feeling of calculated intimacy—or perhaps intimacy was not exactly the right word. It was superficially a platonic affair. No kisses, no embraces and not even a word of endearment. But in spite of the veneer of apparent disinterest Wade was conscious of a distinct mutual magnetism. He and Susan seemed to gravitate naturally towards each other; they possessed a distinct psychological affinity that was satisfying in itself, and as June gave way to July they found themselves spending most evenings in each other's company.

Inevitably, of course, the relationship had to spread to the emotional plane, and in this respect he felt that Susan herself was the principal instigator. The drinks had been holding out well, but inexorably the bottles became empty one by one, and towards the end of the first week in July the alcoholic jaunt came to its end. In the world outside the water ration had been cut to six pints per day, and Wade recognised the utter finality of the last glass of whisky as he and Susan sipped it.

"After this," she said quietly, "there will be no reason for me to come here any more." She was sitting on a chair by the window, looking at him obliquely and enigmatically.

"I guess not," Wade agreed.

"You know, Phil, you're a funny character. I never knew a man to see so much of a girl without making a pass at her."

"Do men still make passes in this topsy-turvy world?"

She smiled grimly. "More than ever, and more insistently. You've seen the crime statistics."

"I wasn't thinking in terms of criminal assault," Wade remarked. "Taking a broad view of human relationships I should have thought that any kind of romantic interest between a man and a woman implied a future of some kind."

"Meaning..."

"Well—surely the future is important to lovers? And since there doesn't seem to be any future worth considering..."

She laughed—a brief, cynical laugh. "You're talking through your hat, Phil. Lovers aren't concerned with the future—only with the present. Wasn't it Freud who said that love is ninety per cent association? Didn't you learn all that during the last war?"

"Maybe you're right at that," Wade conceded.

Susan finished her drink—the final drink—then stood up and placed her glass deliberately on the table. She came over to him, standing quite close, yet in some way remote. There was an archness in her eyes that excited him vaguely.

She said: "I was only teasing, Phil. I understand perfectly that you have a wife and child, so what would you want with a mere youngster like me—especially one that talks too much."

Wade said nothing, holding his glass firmly, and eyeing the remaining contents with bleak indifference.

"I mean—even if you knew that your wife had been sharing her favours with someone else—with, say, a government man—it wouldn't make any difference to you?"

Slowly Wade finished the drink. "You hinted at that once before," he pointed out. "The implication was that Janet knew all about the crisis long before I told her, and that she learned from a man who may have been influential in getting me installed in this I.B.I. job."

"I didn't say so, Phil."

"But you implied it, Sue. How could you know, anyway?"

"I don't know. I have a logical mind—too logical for a woman, perhaps. My father is a government official, and I know about the wire-pulling that has gone on. It just doesn't seem reasonable to me that you could have been appointed to the I.B.I. without a definite motivation."

"Not even the fact that I might be able to do the job efficiently?"

"A thousand journalists could do the job as well, if not better."

"You think there was some influence?"

"I don't know, Phil. Was there?"

He paused to consider. "I got the job, so far as I know, because Stenniger gave me a big build-up with Sir Hubert Piercey."

"Why should he? What did he do for the rest of his staff?"

"Nothing."

She regarded him soberly. "Stenniger is related to Sir Hubert. You knew that, of course."

He shook his head, mildly surprised. "No, I didn't."

"It's a kind of marriage in-law relationship."

"That would account for the leak," Wade murmured thoughtfully. "I always thought it curious that Stenniger should know so much about the impending crisis, and be able to sell out in time to Consolidated Press."

"I imagine Sir Hubert got a percentage on the deal, Phil."

He breathed heavily. "Now you're being really cynical."

"Perhaps I haven't got your faith in human nature."

"I don't know that I've any faith at all in anything. Just what are you suggesting, Sue? That Stenniger got me this job to salve his own conscience because he was having an affair with my wife?"

She looked at him mischievously. "How should I know? At all events Janet is safe and sound in the Arctic. Perhaps it was the least he could do for her."

"I don't believe it," Wade stated decisively.

"It's not even the sort of thing I would want you to believe," she said. "After all, you ought to know your own wife well enough."

"She never had a good word to say for Stenniger."

"Why not? That could have been a defensive attitude, too."

"All right," Wade growled. "You've given me something to think about. I don't believe it, but I'll have to think about it, and when the time comes I'll take it up with Janet. If I may be blunt—I don't think it's any of your business."

"But it is, Phil." She took his arm gently. "You see—I don't want you to base your life on principles that may be false. This may be the end of the world, and neither you nor I might survive it. We know each other pretty well by now. Why don't we do the sensible thing?"

"Such as what?"

"You know damn well what."

"All I know is you seem to be trying to undermine what faith I've got left in the basis of my own married life."

"What married life? To all intents and purposes you're a bachelor, Phil."

"Not in law."

She grimaced briefly. "Does law count for anything any more? It seems to me that every day the world around us is reverting more and more to the fundamental law of nature."

Wade fingered the empty glass, and glanced sorrowfully at the last of the empty bottles. In a sense this was the end of a chapter in itself. The end of the narcotic phase of his life, and the beginning of a more vital facing up to reality and responsibility. He reached out for her, taking her around the waist, and drew her deliberately towards him. She yielded, slowly and deliberately, without change of expression. Presently he was embracing her in a calculated, purposeful manner, and she made no protest.

"We're both logical people, Sue," he said. "That's half the trouble. We put reason before emotion, and we seek emotion on a rational basis."

"Is that so bad?"

"For people like you and me—yes. We're like computing machines, assessing the future in terms of immediate emotional parameters..."

"Why don't you stop talking, Phil. Words are always a barrier in any language."

He kissed her briefly and she responded in the same transient manner. "Neat," she murmured, "but it would hardly disturb the earth in its orbit. Try harder."

He tried harder, and discovered a curious thing—that time came to a halt, and in that interval of silent eternity the earth seemed to stop in its orbit. He allowed himself to dissolve, to become an abstract function of the present moment, the instantaneous present, with no past and no future. And Susan Vance, in all her youth and loveliness, became the only real thing in a world of twisted and distorted shadows.

Later, in the quiet, dark intimacy of the evening, he said softly: "I love you, Sue."

"You don't have to, Phil," she replied. "We're being logical, that's all. You and me, and the pressure of world events. We're not the only ones."

"I guess not."

"And if it hadn't been you, it would have been someone else—perhaps Patten..."

"Isn't that being—just a little too logical?"

She laughed, and a certain quality of harshness in her voice disconcerted him. "Don't try to read between the lines, Phil. There's nothing written there."

"I don't understand."

"It's simple enough. You're trying to look at us in a spiritual way, as if we were the innocent victims of some irresistible romantic urge. It's not like that at all, Phil, and you know it. I'm a methodical scheming character, just like you. You don't need to be spiritual with me—just honest, that's all."

"I'm being honest," said Wade—and, indeed, he meant it.

Wade's infatuation with Susan Vance was a positive thing that obsessed his thoughts day and night, and it was aggravated considerably by her own refusal to accept the situation in any responsible way. They became lovers, amid the typhoid and the cholera and the riots and the peremptory executions of martial law, and yet she never quite gave herself to him—only her body, but nothing of her soul. Even in the act of making love it seemed to him that she was observing from some remote point, dispassionately and almost sardonically. Puzzled and confused, he pursued his own intense emotions with sincere single-mindedness, devoting himself to the girl, and rejecting the jagged memories of Janet that periodically threatened the tranquillity of his mind.

Their relationship was, to a great extent, furtive. During tours of duty they maintained the conventional relations already established between press and cypher departments, and referred to each other by surnames; it was only in the evenings, or during the long exquisite nights, that they abandoned the professional veneer and, in the privacy of their hotel rooms, exploited the lover relationship.

For Wade it was a form of rejuvenation; for the girl, so far as he could judge, a diversion.

He resisted a certain instinctive possessiveness that threatened to poison his attitude towards the girl—threatened to consume him with jealousy whenever he saw her talking to other men, and Patten in particular. He resented the nights when she was on duty in the Cypher Office, and began to hate the circumstances of organisation and duty which kept them apart unnecessarily. And all the time he justified himself in his new-found ardour by recalling the suspicion surrounding Janet and the implication concerning her secret relationship with Stenniger. An eye for an eye, he told himself, and as each day passed, so he became more convinced of his wife's cupidity.

Meanwhile, the outside world became a shambles, maintained in rigorous shape by the ruthless application of military law. Cholera was spreading all over the country—all over Europe. Water stocks reached a new low, sustained only by microscopic injections from the Messiter pipelines, stretching in fine filaments from the solid land surfaces of the British Isles across the dry ocean bed to the residual pools and lakes, and northwards towards the polar ice. But even the pipelines proved to be vulnerable: every day reports arrived in the Cypher Office of attempts to sever them and steal the water being pumped to the central reservoirs. In fact, the Messiter pipelines were never fully operational. Black market gangs were continually engaged in sabotage—cutting the lines and stockpiling water for resale at fabulous prices. As the salt water pools in the Atlantic and the North Sea dried out, so the pipelines became fewer in number, and as July drew to a close, the only effective water supply was that channelled from the north. It was merely a drop in the ocean and was, for the most part, reserved for the use of the armed forces.

Meanwhile, the water ration was cut to three pints per day, and in due course, to two pints. But one could still buy off-ration water on the Black Market at ten shillings a pint. Equally acute was the shortage of food. During the hot rainless summer the green fields of England became brown and lifeless. Cattle were slaughtered from necessity—there were no longer any grazing pastures to sustain them. Wheat stocks were low: no imports were being received from Canada or the U.S.A. Bread was rapidly becoming a luxury.

Despite the absolute embargo on travel, Wade observed from incoming reports that people were moving *en masse* from one part of the country to another, particularly towards the north, into Scotland, and beyond. Aerial photographs revealed that small groups of people were attempting to cross the dry ocean bed north of the Hebrides, pioneering a new route towards the Arctic ice. Wade wondered idly what their ultimate fate would be—probably death from thirst and starvation, or cholera, in the fantastic environment of desiccated sub-oceanic mud and dehydrated undersea flora and fauna. Or, if they ever reached the built-up Arctic zones, death from machine-gun bullets for attempted illegal entry into the haven of security.

The emigration towards the north was to some extent matched by immigration from the south. Across the cracked black trough that was the English Channel came the refugees from the Continent, carrying their few pathetic belongings on their backs, or wheeling their possessions in battered perambulators. They got no further than the barbed wire spanning the south coast of Britain. Machine-gun nests eliminated them with impartial ruthlessness.

Wade was able to witness this for himself one afternoon

during a brief return of Major Carey to his Kingsway base. South of Aldwych a number of buildings had been demolished to make room for a level expanse of concrete that was, in effect, a heliport—a practical landing and take-off zone for helicopters and vertical-ascent aircraft. Carey had apparently returned from the North of England in a helicopter, and, indeed, he was still wearing a flying helmet when he strode into Wade's office. Carey's complexion seemed more florid than ever, and he still wore the same sporty fawn tweeds: he looked as if he had just returned from the Grand National after a major win.

"How're things, Wade?" Carey asked.

Wade shrugged. "A steady decline, I should say—rather like a count-down."

"Count-down to zero? Could be. The sixty-four-dollar question is—when is zero? How soon?"

"A month—two months?"

Carey's moustache quivered interrogatively. "Zero in what respect—or doesn't it matter?"

"It doesn't matter. Zero all round. Water stocks can't be more than three weeks, and once they're gone—well, it's the end. Absolute zero."

Carey blew his nose loudly.

"What I'm wondering," Wade said, "is—have the Cabinet any plans for dealing with the final crisis when it arises in the next few weeks? What's to happen to *us*, and when?"

Carey smiled—a rather twisted smile. "The Cabinet is no longer in this country, so any decisions will probably be quite dispassionate and arbitrary. I believe the official government address is somewhere in Zone D in the Arctic."

"I'm not surprised."

"Not everything goes over the I.B.I. network, Wade. Other countries are playing cagey, too. But don't worry. We shall be looked after—most of us, anyway."

"Most?"

"Wade," Carey said seriously, "it is physically impossible to evacuate every government employee in the time available. The indispensable departments are already in the Arctic. The airlift is going on all the time. But you have to realise that people like us, concerned with information and propaganda, are essentially the rearguard. It is in the public interest that we should remain on duty until the last possible moment."

Wade was vaguely alarmed. "You mean—that some of us may be left behind when the time comes?"

Carey waved a nonchalant hand. "It's on the cards—but not to worry. Things are never so bad as they seem."

"Mm," said Wade thoughtfully. "I sometimes wonder if things aren't worse than we imagine."

Carey lit up a cigarette—luxury indeed—without offering one to Wade. "Things," he said decisively, "are strictly under control. Not in the nicest way, perhaps—but under control. You have to remember that some seventy per cent of the population of this planet is going to die anyway—in the very near future. That changes the moral climate of society. Death is, in a sense, a public service. Even nature realises that. Have you ever thought, Wade, that when mass death is desirable, nature often takes a hand in the proceedings."

"You mean—such things as typhoid and cholera?"

"Exactly."

"I wouldn't blame nature, Major. After all, nature didn't manufacture the H-bomb that split the bed of the Pacific Ocean."

Carey laughed and puffed smoke rings. "Nature manufactured *homo sapiens*, and *homo sapiens* manufactured the H-bomb and destroyed the world. The chain of responsibility is direct enough."

"You're talking in the abstract. But, in fact, every step the government takes is directed towards survival of mankind as a whole."

"Sure, sure," said Carey grinning. "Tell you what, Wade—why don't you come with me on a helicopter trip over the south coast. That way you can see just how the survival programme is working out."

Wade protested at first, but in the end he agreed, partly because Carey was most persuasive in his manner, and partly because he realised that this was in effect his first opportunity to see for himself the physical effects of the water recession. Hitherto his information had been derived from encoded I.B.I. signals, and from official photographs.

He ate a frugal lunch with Major Carey in the Waldorf, but at least it was a lunch, which, he thought, was considerably more than was available to the average citizen outside the governmental barrier. He tried to visualise Shirley Sye in her modest flat, exploiting what assets remained to her in the interests of self-preservation. He recalled that he had promised to send her money and provisions, but that had been an eternity ago, a brittle resolve made in the tension of emotional upset. For all he knew she might even be dead. She was a shadow from a life long since abandoned—a shape of no intrinsic interest, except in retrospect. He dismissed Shirley from his mind and resolved never to think of her again.

After lunch he accompanied Major Carey to the new heliport south of Aldwych. Carey climbed into the pilot's seat, and Wade sat alongside him. The take-off was smooth and competent, and presently the Thames lay beneath them dehydrated into a meandering strip of black clay, with a wisp of stagnant water reflecting the intense blue of the sky like a luminous ribbon.

From the air, London looked normal enough, but here and there Wade could detect the outward symptoms of earthquake damage; across Brixton, for instance, a distinct crevice was visible, cutting obliquely across several blocks of houses, and in certain areas many buildings were empty shells possessing a gutted appearance that reminded him of the last war. The roads were curiously deserted, and the railway tracks were desolate.

Beyond the built-up area, as they flew swiftly towards Sussex and the coast, the open ground formed a dull-brown wasteland reaching to the horizon on all sides. It was as if, Wade thought, an army of flamethrowers had passed through, pursuing a scorched earth policy. The only splashes of green came from the deeply rooted trees—those able to suck the attenuated moisture from the sub-soil and so sustain a mantle of foliage. Dried-out lakes and ponds passed beneath the aircraft—a random succession of dark, shallow craters. If the colour were different it might have been a moonscape—there was the same pervading atmosphere of a stark monochrome wilderness.

Wade failed to recognise the coast when they reached it for the simple reason there was no longer any coast to see. The ground changed colour. A narrow strip of dry sand, yellow, almost white in the sunglare, and then the darker tones of the bed of the English Channel, flung into small undulating ridges, and peppered with stones and boulders and black irregular splashes that might have been masses of dead seaweed. And forlorn hulks that had once been ships lying broken and awry. But no water—only a thin wavering line that gleamed needle-like in the far distance—the final glistening rivulet that was the Channel.

Carey was circling, and presently they were moving back towards the coast. The helicopter lost altitude, and then speed. They were hovering above a strip of sand, and the buildings of a coastal town glowed geometrically about a mile away. Looking down Wade saw barbed wire and military vehicles and concrete pill boxes, and nearer the town, a steel trellis tower bearing a rotating radar aerial.

The helicopter followed the outline of the coast for a few miles. The shadow of the aircraft flitted like a gigantic black moth across the barren ground below. Carey turned to him abruptly and pointed. Following the direction of his arm Wade looked out and down into the grey-yellow of the Channel bed.

He saw tanks—five or six of them—creeping slowly forward across the sunbaked mud and sand, and behind them people—some twenty or thirty—in long straggling lines, following the tanks. Something flashed brilliantly for an instant among the tanks, and smoke billowed outwards, but there was no sound above the throb of the helicopter engine. Wade glanced shorewards and saw the field guns behind the barbed-wire fence, and even as he watched, one of the guns belched smoke, and simultaneously another explosion burst among the tanks.

Fascinated, he witnessed the battle between the invaders from across the Channel and the coastal defenders. Carey's voice resonated crisply in his ears via the intercom.

"This kind of thing goes on all the time. When things get tough the air force intervenes."

"But tanks...?" Wade queried.

"Renegade troops from France or Belgium, followed by hangers-on. They think force of arms will get them through. At least they'll die fighting."

"What would happen if our own troops deserted and became renegades?" Wade asked.

"We may yet find out—the hard way," Carey said enigmatically.

They returned to London and settled down on the bare concrete of the Aldwych heliport. The solid buildings of London seemed to belie the sense of crisis that gnawed at Wade's mind, but the wire barricades at the top of Kingsway were real enough.

He said: "Major Carey—how soon do we pull out of all this?"

Carey eyed him solemnly, pursing his lips. "If we pull out at all, I'd say within three weeks—perhaps less."

Wade nodded silently. Time enough, he thought. It will mean good-bye so far as Sue is concerned, but everything comes to a stop—even the world. We must make the most of our borrowed time, Sue and I, for we have no future together.

He returned to duty in the Consort Building.

X

IT WAS INEVITABLE THAT CHOLERA SHOULD PENETRATE EVEN the defences of the official government zones. The first cases were reported in Whitehall, and then two of the girls in the Filter Room of Consort Building were rushed to an emergency hospital. Cholera was confirmed. Within four days there were eight more cases of cholera, and one of the victims was, ironically, the hale and hearty Major Carey himself. Wade heard the news from a distressed and bewildered Patten.

"Carey's dead," Patten announced hollowly, after entering Wade's office like a ghost. "Cholera," he added briefly in explanation.

Wade sighed. "I'm sorry, Patten. The Major was a good type."

"He had only himself to blame," Patten went on, a little resentfully. "In fact, he may have been responsible for bringing the disease into the government zones."

"You mean because he was always out and about? Carey wouldn't have taken chances."

Patten smiled reluctantly. "Perhaps I knew him better than you, Wade. Officially his job was to liaise with Intelligence units in various parts of the country—secret stuff that couldn't be put over the normal communication channels. But that wasn't enough for Carey. No—there was a bit of the do-gooder in him. He had to mix with the people—to find out for himself just how the individual was coping with events."

"Hardly a crime," Wade observed. "I always suspected that Carey was a genuine humanitarian at heart."

"Oh, he had a big enough heart—too big if you ask me. Things like persuading the commanders of local military units to set up relief centres for civilians—putting troops on half rations to provide field canteens. All done without authority, Wade."

"But he got co-operation from the officers concerned."

"Carey could always talk anyone into co-operating."

Wade lit a cigarette, eyeing Patten thoughtfully, trying to analyse certain conflicting emotional elements in the other man's attitude. Fear was at the root of it, he suspected—not fear of events, or even death, but fear of himself. Patten was behaving like a man whose foundations were subsiding, and the superstructure was beginning to crack.

"If he hadn't been a do-gooder he'd have still been alive," Patten went on, his voice still carrying a curious hint of resentment, not so much a criticism of Carey, but rather an implied sour-grapes attitude that concealed a furtive admiration. There, Wade thought, is the focal point of Patten's fear—it has to do with the morality of being a do-gooder, and he doesn't know whether to raise his hat or spit.

"About four days ago," Patten said, "there was a riot in a hospital near Reading. The hospital was full to capacity with cholera cases, but there were hundreds of hooligans trying to break in..."

"Hooligans?" Wade enquired.

"People with cholera who didn't give a damn for law and order, thinking only of saving their own skins."

"Isn't that what we're all doing in the last analysis?"

Patten laughed shortly. "Not Carey. When the riot got out of control and people started getting killed, including doctors and nurses, the military intervened. So Carey used his influence and got a tented camp set up as an emergency hospital, and personally supervised the medical orderlies for two days, until the War Office clamped down."

"You mean—the tented hospital was closed?"

"Of course. There were no medical supplies. The place was just a collection centre for the dying. You can't risk infecting troops in that way."

"I see," Wade murmured. "Obviously the troops have to be kept fit and healthy to maintain control as the crisis gets worse."

"Exactly. Anyway, that was Carey's lot. He developed cholera in its most acute form. He died this morning."

There was silence for a few moments while the two men looked at each other with expressionless eyes, then Patten continued: "What frightens me, Wade, is that Carey may have been right. I've never felt so confused before. Somehow the outside world hasn't seemed real to us. I never thought of the people out there as human beings—just statistics on paper. I can't help thinking..."

"Why not *stop* thinking," Wade suggested, "then you won't be so confused."

"Because I'm afraid. That's the simple answer. I want to be away from it all—in the Arctic—anywhere. Oh, there has to be a survival group, I know, and those that don't belong to it are as good as dead, so why try to help them? The quicker they die, the better—that's the official attitude. But Carey didn't agree. He was secure enough—one of the group, but something inside him couldn't leave it at that. He had to interfere."

"Maybe Carey had a conscience," Wade said. "Maybe he regarded life as something sacred, beyond all policies and politics. And maybe, in the scheme of things, he didn't consider his own life more important than his principles."

Patten's lip trembled almost imperceptibly. "That's what I was thinking, Wade, and that's what frightens me. If Carey's right, then we're wrong—all of us. How can we in all conscience just sit back and wait for the world to die without so much as raising a finger? And yet I've been smugly pleased to think I was chosen to survive, and now I'm beginning to despise myself for *wanting* to survive."

"You're putting Carey on the level of a martyr," Wade pointed out, "and there's no truth in it. Carey did what he did because that was the way he was made. If you'd been made the same way you'd be out there, too—do-gooding as you call it. But you're different—we're all different."

Patten nodded sadly.

"You're measuring yourself with a yardstick that no longer applies, Patten, and obviously you don't seem to fit. Standards are changing. Your codes of behaviour have to be flexible enough to adapt themselves to changing conditions in the world. You can no more apply the moral code of last year than you could use the standards of, say, a Stone Age man."

Patten wasn't convinced. "If that's true, then it applies to Carey as well."

"Yes—except that Carey's code wasn't flexible enough. He couldn't adapt himself, and now he's dead. Evolution works on that kind of principle."

"You call this evolution?" Patten demanded scornfully. "This deliberate pulling out of a privileged minority behind the guns of an army that doesn't understand what it's all about?"

"They'll understand sooner or later," said Wade, "and then the guns may be pointing our way. I hope we get out in time."

"My God—if only we could get out now," Patten said with passionate feeling. "I can't stand it, Wade—the interminable waiting, the growing realisation that the whole manœuvre is immoral."

"You've got your moralities mixed up," Wade said scathingly. "Why not take a couple of tranquillisers and sleep it off?"

But later, in the silence of his office, Wade realised that Patten had stumbled upon a fundamental truth. There was indeed something false about the crisis through which the world was passing—something criminally false about the way in which mankind had been assigned to two specific camps. False in principle—but principle was abstract. What to do about it?—that was the point. What to do in the here and now. How could any one man hope to fight drought and famine and disease? What could one man's effort do to ward off imminent death on a mass basis? Fantasy, he decided. Patten was neurotic, wallowing in self-recrimination, busily converting the world catastrophe into a personal conflict of conscience. Patten would have to be watched. He was becoming the weak link in the survival chain.

After Carey's death Wade found himself promoted to the full status of Intelligence Officer, but the promotion was meaningless, for the work of the Bureau was beginning to disintegrate. The *National Express* had ceased publication because of the sheer impossibility of adequate distribution, and there had been no issue of *Comment* for several weeks. Furthermore, the international communications network seemed to be in the process of breaking down; many of the I.B.I. stations had gone off the air, and the majority were erratic and unreliable. There were rumours of insurrection and sabotage in various countries, and it appeared to Wade that in the growing crisis the maintenance of channels of communication had a very low priority.

In Britain martial law was reaching an unprecedented degree of applied ruthlessness in an effort to prevent lawlessness and the mass migration of the population. The rationing system, although still officially functioning, had ground to a standstill, for it had become common practice for the strong—and that meant those with arms and weapons—to take what they wanted from the weak. The only reliable sources of food and water were the dispensation centres set up and administered by the military, but they were hopelessly inadequate. A sinister factor began to influence the death statistics: high as were the cholera figures, they were rapidly being overtaken by deaths from thirst and general malnutrition.

Wade's increasing uneasiness was underlined one morning when a message over the intercom asked him to go to Colonel Brindle's office. The Colonel was sitting morosely at his desk, his long jaw sadder than ever. He waved Wade into a chair and said nothing. A few moments later the door opened again and Lieutenant Patten came in. Brindle became more animated.

"Sit down, Patten," Brindle said. "I have asked you both to come here because a policy decision has just arrived from Sir Hubert Piercey's office. I'll be brief. This department will be closing down at short notice in the very near future. The entire staff will fly by helicopter relay to a temporary transit camp near Bletchley, where the I.B.I. transmitters are installed. From there we shall be evacuated to the Arctic, as and when air space is available."

"Excellent," Patten murmured.

Brindle nodded shortly. "I imagined you would be relieved. However, it may not be so easy. You will understand that the fact that we are abandoning our task indicates what I can only describe as the final break-up of civilised order in this country. Until now we have been protected by the military, and the military, I need hardly remind you, have been well looked after. But the supply position is deteriorating, and there have been distinct signs of restiveness among the troops. Yesterday, for instance, air force and army units near Liverpool mutinied and stole six aircraft from Speke airport, presumably in an attempt to fly to the Arctic zones."

"How long can we expect security to hold good, Colonel?" Wade asked.

Brindle shrugged. "Frankly, I don't know. A few days, perhaps. The country's existing water stock is about one week. After that—a mere trickle from the Messiter pipelines, if they survive sabotage."

"Don't you think we ought to get out now, sir?" Patten enquired anxiously.

"All in good time. The process of evacuation is going on all the time. You will understand that there has to be a predetermined order of priority in these things."

"I guess our priority must be rather low," Wade remarked.

"Low enough," Brindle agreed. "And that is a very good reason why the evacuation must take place as quickly and as efficiently as possible, once the movement orders are received."

"When is that likely to be, Colonel?" Wade asked.

"I'm not sure. Two days—perhaps three. In the meantime I think it will be advisable to destroy all documents and code and cypher records and equipment. Superficially there would appear to be no need, but one can never quite foresee the future, and it is wise to leave no evidence behind."

"Evidence?"

"I mean evidence that could be used to show that the government had acted irresponsibly in this crisis. If, for instance, a small group should survive and eventually restore adequate water supplies, they would clearly attempt to seize authority. At a future date the government of this country may wish to return from the Arctic base. There might be conflict, and it will certainly help our case if nothing remains to indicate the way in which the survival programme was decided and carried out."

Wade nodded slowly. "That's a pretty clear admission that they've got a case."

"Of course they've got a case," Brindle said irascibly. "You know that as well as I do. They've got a good case, just like the million Jews that Hitler destroyed in the gas chambers and ovens of his concentration camps. Only he did it positively—we are doing it negatively."

Patten said uneasily: "I'd like to know what is really happening out there—beyond the barricades, among the ordinary men and women and children of London and the world. We've been sheltered from it all. We've built up a picture in our minds from reports and data and statistics. We know as much about the outside world as the average astronomer knows about conditions as they really are on Mars. It's all remote observation and computation and probably far from the truth."

"Sure," Wade remarked sourly. "We, the detached. I'll tell you, Patten—I've had one or two brushes with the outside world as you call it. They weren't pleasant. To hell with the outside world."

Patten frowned and tightened his jaw in protest.

"It's a funny thing," Wade went on, "but there was a time when I deliberately sought to escape from the outside world. I drank heavily. I used alcohol as a protective screen. Now there's no alcohol and I don't need it anyway. There's still the protective screen, and for us life is a quaint dream far removed from the terrible reality. Maybe that's why Sir Hubert picked on me, anyway—maybe he'd figured the way I'd react when the crisis really broke."

"Maybe he also figured you'd fall in love with Susan Vance," Patten suggested acidly.

Wade scowled. "Maybe you should mind your own business."

Colonel Brindle tapped politely on the desk with his knuckles. "Relax, gentlemen. This is neither the time nor the place for personal feuding. Anyway, Wade is right. The outside world has changed considerably. It has become alien to us, and we are no longer of it. Incredible things are happening. You think, perhaps, that rape and murder are the ultimate sins. I can tell you this—in certain parts of Europe where drought and famine have reached desperate proportions there are authenticated reports of cannibalism. It's only a matter of time before that kind of thing starts happening over here. Before the end there will be a Black Market in human blood to drink and human flesh to eat. The community will dissolve into tribes, preying on each other. Mankind will revert to the animal phase, and a million years of evolution will have evaporated completely."

"I can't believe it," Patten said sullenly. "It will never be as bad as that. In the end there will still be courage and human dignity, and people will die honourably."

Brindle's lips moved slowly into a thin, twisted line. "People will die honourably when they have a future to die for, when they can sacrifice their lives to preserve and protect all that they cherish. They will die honourably if their minds are free from the stress of thirst and hunger. Those conditions don't apply, Patten. There is no future for them, and their courage can preserve and protect nothing, and in the long run deprivation and malnutrition will turn them all into desperate beasts. And we can do nothing about it—except save ourselves."

"In all conscience—have we the right to save ourselves?" Patten demanded hollowly.

"I'm afraid conscience has very little to do with it," Brindle pointed out. He stood up and came over to the two men, regarding them with a certain fixed melancholy. "Take my advice. Be circumspect. Treat the people out there"—and he waved one hand vaguely at the wall—"as an enemy. In the long run that is exactly what they are, and they may yet stand between us and safety."

Wade nodded in agreement, but Patten was lost in a subdued mood of gloomy introversion.

The next day Susan Vance came into Wade's office, closed the door quietly, kissed him lightly and said: "Do you love me, Phil?"

"You know I do."

She held on to him for a moment. "What's going to happen to us in the next few days? I've heard about the evacuation. I've been worrying ever since."

Wade embraced her gently. "I thought we'd agreed to be logical about everything, Sue. Borrowed time, remember?"

"I'm trying to be logical, darling, but it's so hard."

Wade released her and sat on the corner of his desk. "I wish to God I had a cigarette," he said vehemently. "And a bottle of Scotch."

"I take it they'll send you back to your wife and son."

"That would seem to be the official procedure."

"Do you want to go back?"

Wade did not answer immediately.

"Why can't we stay together?" she asked. "Does everything have to come to a stop because our work here is finished?"

"I don't know," said Wade. "I've been very happy here with you. And in a way that seems wrong in itself. What right has anyone to happiness in a world on the brink of annihilation? Aren't there some things more important than the pursuit of happiness?"

"What things?" she asked desolately.

"Again I don't know, Sue. Can we afford to have a sense of responsibility—of duty?"

"We can't afford luxuries, Phil. Time is too short."

"But *are* they luxuries?"

"They must be if you have a wife who was unfaithful…"

Wade sighed wearily. "I'm sorry, Sue, but I can't believe it somehow. I've thought about it seriously. But Janet and Stenniger—it's just impossible."

"You think I invented it?"

"I didn't say that."

"But it's there, in your mind. I invented it to set you against Janet, to make things easier for me."

He crossed to her and took her arms. "Sue, you've got the wrong angle on things. I haven't made up my mind about anything. I'll find out the truth from Janet when I see her again—if I see her again. In any case, even if she is guilty, it cancels out. I made a mistake myself once—a long time ago. I'm trying to live in the present, and that's all we can do, any of us. Let's face the future when it comes, Sue."

She inclined her head in solemn acquiescence.

"Meanwhile," he went on, "there are still a few days left to us. And, if things work out that way, maybe we'll stay together for a long time to come."

"I don't like the way you say maybe," she murmured, smiling ruefully, "but if you love me—well, that's all that matters."

"I love you," he said.

They kissed again, more intently, and when it was over Susan detached herself from his embrace and walked across the room, keeping her back towards him.

"I'm scared and unsettled, Phil. I need reassuring. That's why I had to come and see you."

"Anything wrong?" he asked.

She turned to face him abruptly. "Well, in the first place I'm pregnant—at least, I think I am."

I'm not surprised, Wade was about to say, but thought better of it. He went over to her and took her hand. "That makes a difference, Sue," he said.

"Why should it?"

"Oh—you know me. I've got a thing about responsibility."

"Phil—I didn't choose to be pregnant in order to get a hold on you."

He smiled. "I know, honey. But now that you've got a hold—I think I rather like it."

That pleased her as it was meant to, but in a moment her expression became solemn again.

"Phil—I've been selfish. I've talked about myself. More important things are happening around us."

"More important?"

"Yes. I don't know if you've heard about Lieutenant Patten…"

"No."

"Last night he committed suicide. Just—hanged himself—in his room at the Waldorf."

Wade stared at her aghast for a moment. "But why…?"

"I don't know. For a long time he's been strange in his manner—introspective and embittered."

Wade recalled Patten's resentful attitude of the previous day and remembered the distinct evidence of an outraged conscience. Patten had been too sensitive; he had not been able to adapt himself to the rapidly changing environment. A phrase from the far past re-echoed in his mind—the general adaptation syndrome—the desensitising of the individual in a time of crisis. Well, Patten had missed the syndrome all right, while all around him the entire world was busy jumping on the syndromic wagon and desensitising itself like hell. He felt sorry for Patten, but recognised the abstract justice of his fate.

"I think I know why," he said. "Towards the end Patten had conscience trouble. He seemed unable to reconcile the idea of deliberate and unscrupulous governmental survival tactics with the inevitable fate of the mass of humanity. He had principles, and in this day and age principles are obsolete. He was a misfit."

"You're probably right," Susan admitted quietly. "I'm afraid I didn't care much for Patten, though he knew his job. But I'm sorry just the same."

"Maybe he's better off. Maybe we'll envy him in the course of time."

"I can't believe that," she said. After a pause she continued: "There's one disturbing item of news. A serious fire has broken out in the East Ham area. During the night the government allocated one thousand gallons of water in an attempt to keep the fire under control, but by the time they got the bowsers and pumps into position the fire had spread and the water was worse than useless."

"So—what happened...?"

"The fire is spreading. The last report, half an hour ago, put the flame front at Mile End—up as far as Leyton and beyond. With the wind stiffening from the east the fire is advancing quickly towards the City."

"Sounds serious," Wade commented.

"It's worse than that, Phil. Everything is tinder dry, and there's no water. They're using explosives to demolish houses at Bethnal

Green to try to check it, but the reports are sketchy and very much delayed."

Wade pursed his lips thoughtfully. "Funny thing how history repeats itself. I mean—the Black Death—cholera in London, and the Great Fire of London in 1666. It's all happening over again, only this time on a much grander scale, and with no possibility of any kind of future."

"The casualties are heavy," Susan said. "Two hospitals were gutted before they could get the patients out."

"What are the prospects?"

"Either they'll control the fire with explosives, or it will continue to spread while the wind keeps up. It may even reach us here."

"That might be a blessing. It would certainly precipitate the matter of evacuation for us."

She looked at him ruefully. "I agree so much, Phil, but it still sounds callous when you say it that way."

"Not callous—just objective. We might put it to Brindle that there's a strong case for jumping the gun."

"The Colonel has to obey orders."

"I'm beginning to wonder why. In fact I'm beginning to wonder whether anyone has the right to give orders under present-day conditions."

She placed a restraining hand on his arm. "That's the kind of attitude we're supposed to be fighting, Phil—the mood of anarchy—indiscipline. At the first sign of mutiny in any of us we'd be thrown to the wolves on the other side of the barricades."

He took her hand in his and squeezed it amiably. "Maybe you're right, Sue. In any case, there's not much danger of mutiny. They picked their types too well. Most of us have remained consistently unmoved by the whole bloody business."

"Except Patten."

"He was unmoved enough, but in the end broke down under the strain."

"I suppose you're right. Do you think there's any danger that we might break down too in time, Phil?"

Wade took her in his arms for a few moments. "Individually we might, but together—no. Not while we can hold on to each other and shut out the world from time to time. That way we stay sane."

"I like staying sane that way," she murmured.

Presently she returned to her office.

Later in the morning Wade checked over Patten's office to familiarise himself with the general trend of recent work, for it seemed unlikely that a replacement Cypher Officer would be available for some days, if at all. Due to the deterioration of international communications, the pressure on the cypher department had decreased considerably, and Wade thought it probable that the existing staff would be able to cope with the remaining work for the next few days—possibly up to the date of the final evacuation, which could not now be long delayed.

In a drawer in Patten's desk he came across a diary—a small hard-cover notebook in which the pages were crammed with minute but carefully executed handwritten notes. It was not a diary in the conventional sense, for there were no dates—rather was it an informal book of comment and private observation.

Wade glanced through it hastily, not wishing to pry, but curious to learn whether Patten had recorded the reasons for his act of suicide. A reference to himself caught his eye, and he read:

This man Wade is an opportunist, and so is Susan Vance. They both have in common a certain methodical amorality—the kind that is so common in this day and age. I won't deny an element of jealousy. Susan is a fascinating young woman, and I too have had my dreams, and my regrets. But how empty it all seems now.

There followed a few paragraphs of a rambling personal nature, and then: *The Philip Wades and the Susan Vances of the world are the insensitive ones, living in the circumscribed world of their own narrow thoughts and feelings. They'll get by, because they will never see the larger issues involved. Right and wrong for them is what they like and what they don't like. They are the kind that would bless the horror that has thrown them together, seeing no further than their own selfish urges.*

Wade smiled sourly. Patten was entitled to his own personal opinions. He turned the pages until he came to the final entry.

There is no other possible interpretation. The mechanism of the survival group is an evil thing. God knows I wanted to survive, but I am one among millions. People like Brindle and Wade accept their right to live as a divine privilege, accepting it without question, as I once did. It took Carey to destroy my complacency—to show me that I'm on the wrong side of the fence. It's a thing I can't dismiss, nor have I the courage to do anything about it. They chose me as a non-reacting type, but in the end I reacted, and I see now that I have failed myself, and failed humanity. I wanted escape, but there is no escape from what is already done. All that remains is oblivion.

Wade closed the book pensively. Funny how a rational character like Patten could yield so swiftly and tragically to a feeling of obsessive remorse. He began to understand more clearly Sir Hubert Piercey's object in specifying the psychological make-up of the people required to serve in the survival group. But even he couldn't foresee changes in personality—even he couldn't accurately predict the breaking strain of any one individual.

It gets you one way or the other, Wade supposed. Once the neutral psychology collapses you veer towards the good or the evil. You become pious and conscience-ridden, or you shed the veneer of humanity and become ruthless and brutal. Either way means destruction, and the only salvation lies in preserving the fine balance of the mind—to accept both the good and the bad without reaction, to follow a predetermined course like an automaton, suppressing the finer feelings, denying the existence of injustice and shame and horror and inhumanity, seeing the picture as a whole, as a pattern in the temporal evolution of the planet, an impersonal cross-section of a moment in time. In a hundred years from now it will all be history, he thought, and I shall be no better and no worse than Patten, for all his soul searching.

He replaced the diary in the drawer of the desk, resolving to give it to Colonel Brindle later that day.

In the early afternoon Wade and Susan Vance went on to the roof of the Consort Building to join some two dozen other members of the staff who were viewing the distant smoke pall over East London. The panorama was depressing, and the smoke haze was thick enough to make the air pungent to breathe. Towards the East End the sky was a leaden grey with a hint of orange glow reflecting from the smoke cloud near the horizon.

As he watched Wade saw three distinct flashes of amber light beyond the skyline. Seconds later came a remote multiple concussion like the distant blast of anti-aircraft shells.

"Dynamiting in progress," Susan remarked.

"And not too far away," Wade added. "Certainly nearer than Bethnal Green."

"How near?"

"Difficult to say exactly. The City—Aldgate—perhaps nearer—as near as St. Paul's."

She took his arm and clung to him. "If things were that bad they wouldn't allow us to stay here."

Thoughtfully Wade stared into the black and orange haze. "It could be that they don't know. Communications don't seem to be very reliable." A moment later, in a voice that implied decision, he added: "I'm going to take a look for myself."

She reacted in alarm.

"Don't worry, honey. I'm not going to mix with the wolves. I'll use a helicopter." Noting her lack of comprehension, he went on: "A quick trip over the fire zone. It's the only way to get accurate information."

"Phil," she said anxiously, "a helicopter isn't a bomber, and it's a long, long time since you ever flew a plane."

"I flew a helicopter a few times in the final year of the war. I know the ropes."

"Won't you need to get Colonel Brindle's permission?"

He squeezed her arm reassuringly. "There are times in life, Sue, when it's more expedient to take small matters like permission for granted."

"Then take me with you."

"No," he said firmly.

"Why not, Phil—because it's dangerous?"

"There's no danger. It's just that—well, what I'm going to do may be regarded as a breach of discipline. Better for one of us to risk censure than two."

"I'm not worried about censure," she insisted. "I want to come with you."

In the end, because she flatly refused to be left behind, he consented, and around three o'clock they left the building as unobtrusively as possible and made their way towards the Aldwych heliport.

There were, in fact, four helicopters on the concrete landing ground, and the area was fenced off and adequately guarded. Wade and the girl had to identify themselves before they were admitted, and they promptly made their way towards the small control tower overlooking the port. The Controller was a small sleepy-eyed man with dark tousled hair. He glanced up briefly as they entered the control room, then carried on writing something on a sheet of printed paper.

He said: "Yes?"

"I'm Philip Wade, I.B.I. Intelligence Officer. This is Miss Vance of Cyphers."

The Controller looked up without much interest.

"I want a helicopter for about half an hour. Colonel Brindle thinks it might be a good idea to get a bird's-eye view of the fire."

The Controller shrugged. "You got a written authorisation?"

"No—but you can check with the Colonel."

The Controller lifted the phone and began to dial.

Wade said: "You won't be able to get the Colonel right now. He went over to Whitehall."

Slowly the Controller replaced the phone, eyeing Wade doubtfully, but not suspiciously. "It's irregular, Mr. Wade, but if Colonel Brindle said so, then it's okay by me. Better take B for Baker. She's fuelled up and ready for take-off."

"Thanks," said Wade.

"Half an hour, you said?"

"That's right."

They left the control tower and walked across to the helicopter with the scarlet B beneath the I.B.I. insignia. He helped Susan into the tiny compartment and took his place in the pilot's seat. Although the controls differed from those he had seen and used during the war, he had taken the opportunity to study them during his recent trip to the south coast with the deceased Major Carey, and they were now familiar enough. He started the rotor leisurely, making each step of the pre-flight preamble with careful precision. The girl watched him with mild interest, but her thoughts were remote.

"It would be nice," she said quietly, "if we were leaving London for ever. Now, I mean, in this helicopter. Just you and me, flying to the Arctic zone."

"This old bus would never make it," Wade commented. "She doesn't carry enough fuel."

"There's no harm in wishing."

"I guess not."

His hand moved on the controls and the noise of the engine surged in pitch and volume, and the concrete slipped away from beneath them. The control tower was already falling obliquely and diminishing in size. It became a toy building among the many toy buildings of the Aldwych area, and the dry sombre bed of the Thames curved sullenly to the south.

Wade took the machine up to a thousand feet, then hovered for a while to get his bearings. From this altitude he could see the fire—not in so many distinct flames, for visibility was poor, but as an undulating orange glare beyond the dome of St. Paul's cathedral, in the direction of Liverpool Street. The smoke was drifting beneath them now, riding the wind, and obscuring the finer detail of the maze of streets below. His hand moved on the controls, and the machine moved gently towards the distant fire.

It was worse than he had imagined. From a hover point above Mansion House, beyond St. Paul's, he could see the perimeter of the blaze, flickering in gigantic tongues of fire over Moorgate and northwards towards Old Street and City Road. Liverpool Street was already engulfed, it seemed, as was the heart of the City, centring on Bank and Monument. The black belching smoke turned day into night, so that the streets below became lost in the swirling gloom. He reduced altitude, descending to five hundred feet, then four hundred, until it became possible to perceive what should have been Cannon Street, but the thoroughfare had lost all shape, and was part of a wilderness of shattered masonry and concrete stretching beyond the limits of visibility to the north and south. High explosives had obviously done their job well, but even so Wade found himself doubting whether the man-made desolation of razed buildings would prove an effective barrier; indeed, so far as he knew there had been other barriers, further to the east, and yet the fire was advancing.

He flew the helicopter towards the north, keeping the flame front within clear visibility and maintaining an altitude of four hundred feet. Immediately below the desolation continued, cutting across the built-up area of streets and houses in a broad ribbon of rubble some two hundred yards wide. At Essex Road the demolition came to its end, and here Wade was disconcerted to note that the fire had already outflanked the blown-up zone.

He dropped lower to observe more clearly if there were any human activity in the roads below, but the vertical viewpoint was deceptive. Something was moving at speed along Essex Road—probably a military truck—but there was no sign of people, no sign of evacuation or of the movement of population. He assumed that any necessary evacuation had already taken place, but at the same time he could not suppress a suspicion lurking in the dark depths of his mind that perhaps no attempt at evacuation had been made whatever; it might even be that authority had decreed that, in cholera-ridden London, any decrease in the population was bound to be a good thing.

"I think we ought to go back," came Susan's voice over the intercom.

Wade nodded without answering. Something within him responded to the depressed anxiety in the girl's voice. It wasn't good to be outside the barrier and away from the security of the government zone. Consort Building and the Waldorf were located at the still calm centre of the hurricane and it was a bad thing to be detached from that point of self-preservation, even in a helicopter at three hundred feet above ground level. The outer world had all the appearance of hell—it was an ugly, bitter, devastated world, and its denizens were unseen, as if they had taken to living underground. Mentally he consigned it to the flames, hoping at the same time that Colonel Brindle had been able to do something about expediting the evacuation from Kingsway before the hungry flames roared into Fleet Street and High Holborn.

His hand tightened on the control lever, about to climb away from the crushed remains of smoking London, and in that same instant the ground north of Essex Road exploded into sudden incandescent fury. Wade froze, astounded, and Susan's fingers clutched at his arm.

As he watched the ground seemed to rise up on a tidal wave of liquid fire. Buildings disintegrated into jagged fragments, arcing and weaving, silhouetted blackly against the angry orange background. The glow faded, and a moment later the blast wave seized the helicopter and shook it turbulently. Debris clattered on the dural of the fuselage and ricocheted from the whirling blades of the rotor. Susan screamed shrilly in the intercom.

"It's all right," Wade said urgently, fighting the sickness that threatened to twist his abdomen into paralysis. "It's all right, Sue. Just demolition work. We got a bit too close."

It was over. The high explosives had done their job and the debris was falling torrentially back to the ground. The helicopter was swamped in soaring black smoke, and all sight had disappeared beyond the reinforced glass of the windows, some of which were starred and semi-opaque from the impact of flying masonry.

He switched on the cabin light and glanced reassuringly at Susan's white face. She made a thin smile, frightened and unconvinced. He looked at the instruments. The altimeter needle was moving slowly, creeping downwards towards zero. He pulled on the control column and cut in the auxiliary boost, but the engine merely shuddered, and presently he realised that something was seriously wrong—uncontrollably wrong. Damage, perhaps, to the rotor, or to the engine itself... At all events the machine was losing altitude, slowly but steadily.

The smoke was still about them and he could see nothing, but he made a computation and turned towards the west, as he visualised it. He stared in fascination at the altimeter—one-eighty feet—one seventy—one sixty...

"Sue, honey..." he said. "We're not going to make it. We're going to crash..."

Her voice was strained and toneless. "Please try, Phil. Please try..."

"I'll do my best. With luck we ought to get as far as High Holborn. If I can put her down gently we'll be able to walk back to Kingsway…"

The smoke cleared quite suddenly, and there, not more than ten feet below the helicopter, were the flat roofs of tall buildings. Desperately Wade manipulated the controls, but the buildings rose stubbornly towards them, and long before he reached it he recognised the point of impact as a concrete parapet adjoining a row of chimney stacks adorned with forlorn, twisted television aerials.

The shock of the collision was less than he had anticipated. For a brief instant he thought it would be all right—that the machine would simply grind to a halt among the chimney stacks and aerials, but he had underestimated the speed of descent. The helicopter smashed its way through the stacks, spinning and lurching wildly, then hurtled broadside against a massive stone coping at the edge of the roof. It tilted. The rotor threshed the air then struck brickwork and disintegrated. A moment later the crippled aircraft had fallen over the edge of the roof towards the road some ten storeys below.

The final drop lasted for a small eternity. Wade reached out for Susan, but she was slumped over her seat and appeared to be unconscious. He grappled with the controls for the last time. And then the world dissolved in a confusion of noise and blinding light.

XI

SOMEBODY HAD LIFTED HIS HEAD AND ALLOWED IT TO DROP back on to a hard surface. Pain burned throughout his body. His legs were twisted beneath him and were quite numb from below the knees. Pungent air irritated his nostrils, air tainted with acrid smoke and swirling heat, and voices made sounds in the air, but the sounds were meaningless.

He opened his eyes with considerable effort and found himself looking through a mass of distorted metal and broken glass towards a dark brooding sky crawling with streamers of angry smoke. The voices came more sharply to his ears, and, turning his head painfully, he observed khaki-clad figures moving over bent and broken fragments of dural. The figures were manhandling a limp human shape that looked vaguely familiar, though the identity escaped him for the moment.

Fragments of conversation began to take on meaning.

"The man's alive but unconscious."

"Leave him for now. The girl's more important."

"Down here. I'll check her over."

"Right arm looks pretty shapeless."

"It's broken. May be crushed ribs, too. Pity—she's a good looker, and young enough."

"She's all right from the waist down, isn't she?"

"We can soon find out."

"Joe, there isn't time for what you've got in mind. It'll take twenty minutes to get the H.E. chain wired up. Best thing we can do is finish them both off and get the job done. The fire's getting too close as it is."

"Don't be a damn pessimist, Bill. We can be through with her in a few minutes—all of us. How about that church hall over there? Nice and private like."

"All right, but we'll have to make it quick."

The figures had picked up the shape and were carrying it across the roadway, Wade saw. The shape was a girl and recognition seeped sluggishly into his brain. It was Susan Vance, of course. For a long time he was unable to understand what was happening, or what Susan was doing in the hands of half a dozen soldiers. And then the bombshell exploded in his mind, and terror and anger ran wild in his arteries.

Momentarily lost in an unreasoning panic, he pushed himself stiffly to his feet, but his numb legs collapsed immediately, and he fell among the twisted ruin that had been the helicopter. Again he stood up, holding on to a jagged spar for support, then thrust himself forward.

"Stop!" he shouted. "Stop!"

The soldiers stopped and looked round. One of them walked slowly back towards him, swinging a rifle by its strap. A young fellow, tall and lithe, but with brutality in his narrow eyes.

"What's the beef, chum?" the soldier asked mildly.

"Leave her alone," Wade said fiercely. "Go back and tell them to leave her alone."

The soldier grinned amiably. "You wouldn't want to spoil a bit of harmless fun, would you, chum? Share and share alike these days, you know. Besides, we don't see many women—they keep themselves hidden away, 'specially the young ones…"

"In the name of humanity…" said Wade.

"Out of date, aren't you, chum? There ain't been no humanity round these parts for a long time. You take what you can get when you can get it."

"Look," said Wade in desperate appeal, "she's hurt—badly hurt. She needs medical care..."

"Sure—she's got a broken arm. She ain't likely to put up much of a fight. And as for medical care—there isn't any. The hospitals are full. We've orders to shoot serious casualties to save them suffering."

The soldiers were moving on again, carrying Susan's inert body. Wade reached out for the other man's arm, but he backed away suspiciously, raising the rifle.

"I know a place," Wade said urgently. "In Kingsway—not far from here. If you'll help me get her back there..."

"You talk too much, chum," said the soldier. He took the rifle by the barrel and swung it. The butt caught Wade on the side of the head, hurling him into the dural and glass debris, where he lay still.

The soldier then reversed the rifle and aimed it at his victim, but an abrupt scream from the other side of the road drew his attention. He glanced back. The group were at the entrance to the church hall, and from this distance it seemed to him that the girl had regained consciousness. There appeared to be some kind of struggle taking place.

He slung the rifle over his shoulder and ran to join in the fun.

"Hold it!"

The terse command penetrated the pain and confusion of Wade's mind in an immense authoritative voice. He fought to regain the stability of his senses, to disperse the dark agonising cloud that veiled his eyes. The soldiers were standing in a motionless group, and another figure was advancing from a gloomy side street—a burly, khaki-clad figure wearing chevrons and carrying a sub-machine gun in an enormous hand.

Slowly, like some kind of inhuman automaton, Wade dragged himself across the jagged wreckage of the helicopter. The left side of his face was swollen and the bones of his jaw ached with every movement of his mouth. He brushed his cheek with a hand, and looked at the blood on his fingers without reaction. There was a chill ice in his brain and a passionate loathing for the men in uniform who had taken Susan Vance away—a loathing that extended far beyond the point of focus to embrace all troops and all people of this, the sub-human world beyond the barrier.

The fire seemed nearer than ever; beyond the rooftops sparks drifted and danced in the writhing smoke, and the roar of the flames was the sound of a hungry furnace. He looked towards the khaki group by the church hall, then cautiously picked himself up and limped unsteadily from the debris. In a moment the big newcomer was holding his arm, supporting him roughly. Wade found himself looking into the red, exasperated but not unkindly face of a sergeant.

"Bloody civilians," said the sergeant with considerable feeling. "As if we haven't got enough trouble!" Then, turning to the others: *"Put her down!"*

They laid the body of Susan Vance on the grey concrete slabs of the pavement. She moved spasmodically, groaning a little. Their eyes were sullen and resentful, but they had not yet lost all respect for authority.

"We were only going to find somewhere to make her comfortable…" murmured a subdued voice. The sergeant laughed cynically.

"A likely bloody story!" He swung the sub-machine gun with facile competence. "You think this is some kind of spree? A free for all? Well, you're wrong!" He turned abruptly to Wade. "You with her?"

Wade nodded.

The sergeant took a deep breath. "You ought to be hanged, mate, bringing a woman out in this lot."

Wade indicated the remains of the helicopter. "We were flying over the fire zone. Got caught by... blasting. She's hurt bad."

"Where are you from?" demanded the sergeant.

"Information office—Government zone..."

The sergeant uttered an obscenity. He glared balefully at Wade. "Why the hell don't you keep out of it, mate? You can't help. Don't you know that? I've got a platoon of good men, but they've taken a big knock, and there ain't much gallantry left in them. They're no different from anyone else these days. They don't take kindly to government types, and they go crazy at the sight of a woman, whether she's hurt bad or not. We've got a job to do—demolition and destruction. That kind of thing gets a hold of you. Nothing's important any more, and nothing matters. All we want is to be left to get on with the job."

"All right," Wade said wearily. "I have to get her back to Kingsway. I'll need help."

"I wouldn't trust any one of them to help you, mate. Bloody conditions breed bloody behaviour."

"Then we'll make our own way..."

"And the best of luck, mate. It's a good job I came on the scene. Another N.C.O. would have had you both shot, but I'm a family man. Wife and six kids up in Rutland—still alive, though God knows how. That's why I like to keep my hands clean."

"Thanks," Wade said simply, but the sergeant scowled.

"Clear out," he ordered. "Take her and clear out, mate. We're blasting in a few minutes. And if ever you make it, keep your fingers crossed for Sergeant Slade. Now clear out."

Clumsily, aware of his tremendous physical weakness, Wade helped Susan Vance to her feet. She was hardly conscious, and only capable of slight effete movements. Under the narrow surveillance of the silent troops he dragged her along the pavement, away from the fire, in the direction of Kingsway. The voice of the sergeant sounded remotely in his ears, issuing incomprehensible orders. Thank God for the sergeant, he thought, holding the girl tightly. Thank God for a human being.

It was the contrast that paralysed his thinking, he realised. The overpowering sense of evil, and the small but potent element of goodness; the slender balance between sadistic brutality and human dignity—or was that the wrong term to use at this time and place? They are the enemy, he thought, but they're not all the same. One good man had the power to restore sanity—or was it sanity? Perhaps they were simply afraid of him—of the three chevrons, of the air of authority, of the sub-machine gun. Perhaps it was just a question of time—in a day or two the sergeant himself might revert to the level of the others. In a decaying world there was nothing but decay. But here and now there was still a spark of humanity to illuminate the spiritual darkness.

It had become all too obvious that the girl couldn't make it; she was sagging in his arms and dragging her feet along the ground, and for all he knew she was unconscious. In a sudden surge of desperate strength he picked her up bodily, and staggered forward, then caught sight of her broken arm lying twisted and grotesque across her body. An irrational logic possessed his tormented mind—he realised suddenly and obsessively that he would have to do something about it. Already the flesh around the fracture was purple and swollen.

He turned abruptly into a side street and put her down in the doorway of a derelict office block, propping her against the rough grey concrete of the wall.

"Sue," he said, slapping her cheek gently. "Sue."

She opened her eyes mechanically; there was no intelligence in them.

"This is Phil. I'm going to leave you for a moment. I've got to find something to fix that arm of yours with."

There was no reaction or response.

Quickly he glanced round. The street was drab and desolate. It was as if every human being had been evacuated from the area—and that, he realised with a shock, was probably the truth. For all he knew the street beneath and around him might be dynamited into complete disintegration at any instant as part of the fire-fighting procedure.

Viciously he kicked at the door of the office block, but it was securely bolted from the inside. He moved round to the windows, observing that the panes of glass had been broken and shattered already, perhaps by the blast of recent explosions. Cautiously he swung himself on to the sill of a ground floor window, and eased himself through the jagged periphery of the broken glass hole. At least his needs were simple enough—some lengths of rigid wood—desk rules if it came to the point. With the aid of his shirt he could fix up a splint and protect Susan's broken arm from further damage.

But the rooms were empty, with no furniture or fittings, and even the floor coverings had been stripped. With a sense of increasing panic he ascended the spiral stairs to the second and third storeys, but there was nothing. From a fragmented window at the rear of a building he found himself looking down into a small courtyard in which was a rusted, useless car and a wooden crate. Triumph leaped momentarily in his veins.

He rushed headlong down the stairs and crashed through a flimsy basement door into the courtyard. The crate was empty, but strongly built. Quickly he looked around for some kind of tool with which to dismantle it. In the car, perhaps...

But the car was a mere shell from which the seats and instruments and most of the engine had been stripped. He tugged vainly at the front bumper, hoping to dislodge it, but it remained stubbornly fixed to the chassis. When he abandoned the attempt his hands were brown with flaking rust.

The outside door to the courtyard was open, and he passed through it into another silent street. Somewhere, he thought, there must be a heavy object—even a brick. Time was running out, and he could not afford to leave the girl alone for much longer. He began to run along the street towards a cross-road—and suddenly he was back in High Holborn.

He made a quick computation, checking his sense of direction. Better get back to Susan first, then make a final assault on the crate. Quickly he walked to the next turning.

A whistle sounded remotely. He looked up towards the smoke-swollen sky livid with the orange glow of the great fire, and a cold twisting fear began to curl in his abdomen. This isn't real, he told himself. It could never come to this. All the genius and ingenuity of mankind—could never let things go this far. It was all a nightmare and they would awake in the calm security of Kingsway...

He rounded the corner, his heart throbbing uncontrollably. Susan was still there, where he had left her, half sitting, half lying, in the angle of the doorway. As he hurried towards her the distant whistle sounded again.

A curious thing happened. The entire street rose into the air on a cushion of roaring fire and his body rose and spun in an agonising whirling jig as the entire world exploded.

His body was stiff and cold, as if already set in *rigor mortis*, and a great weight bore down on him, and there was the stench of death in his nostrils. The air throbbed with distant explosions and somewhere remote a siren wailed forlornly. He opened his eyes but could see nothing immediately recognisable: around him and below him and on top of him were curious inert shapes in white and pink and crimson.

He turned his head and found himself looking into a dead face with frosted eyes and gaping mouth. The eyes bored sightlessly into his and the stiff lips were crusted with dark dried blood. He saw long brown hair tangled and clotted, and realised with a shock that the face was that of a woman.

Slowly he gained a sense of orientation and began to perceive the detail of his environment, and as his knowledge grew so his sense of horror increased. He was buried in a pyramid of naked corpses, one of a hundred or more bodies, male and female, piled in the centre of a wide road that might have been High Holborn or Oxford Street. The weight of the bodies pinned him down and paralysed his movements, but gradually, with agonising slowness, he was able to extricate his arms, and so wriggled free from the mound of death. He rolled over icy rigid limbs and torsos to the ground where he lay for several minutes, recouping his energy.

And then, recalling recent events, he marvelled that he was still alive. He was completely naked, and his body bore the ugly marks of violence. Clotted blood stained his shoulder and his thigh. He inspected the wounds and realised, with a sense of irony, that he had escaped with flesh lesions—no more, no less. His left arm was sluggish and painful, but he was able to use his right arm effectively.

He looked around the deserted road and saw a further pile of bodies about a hundred yards away. The sky was dark, and not only because of the smoke; evening and night were already casting their veil over the horrors of London town. The fire glowed dull orange over the rooftops and its unceasing roar echoed in his ears like surf on a beach.

Funeral pyres, he thought. The facile disposal of the dead. They thought I was dead, too, but I tricked them. Or, rather, fate tricked them. I'm not dead, yet—but I'm not far from it. What's to happen? The fire will pass this way and cremate the dead—or are there high explosives planted into this very road, destined to disintegrate everything into a common rubble of concrete fragments and shattered protoplasm?

Not all of the bodies were naked, he observed. Some still wore their own shabby clothing, and their drawn lifeless faces bore the imprint of disease—of cholera. He shuddered involuntarily, and shivered from cold. He needed clothing, and he knew what he had to do.

He spent a long time selecting his attire, as one might ponder the wares on a bargain counter, and presently, realising that there was no time to waste, he robbed a corpse of a grey shirt and brown denim trousers and worn black shoes. Cholera infected, without a doubt, he told himself, but it didn't seem to matter. He was dressed and respectable—as respectable as a scarecrow, with all the energy of a deflated balloon, but he was alive—for the moment.

Susan might be there, he realised suddenly. She might be there, among those bodies, lying twisted and stiff in death, awaiting the devouring flames. She would almost certainly be there. She might be any one of them, for they all looked alike, and in death they had lost their individuality. He hadn't the courage to look for her. He turned his back on the pyramid and made his way haltingly away from the direction of the fire.

The pain he did not mind—it was to be expected—but the weakness that made him stumble and fall every few yards infuriated him. He cursed the incompetence of his legs, and fought the faintness that hovered at the back of his mind like a black cloud, ready to swoop upon him at any moment to destroy his consciousness. Be logical, he told himself. Be rational. Think, step by step. First—Susan is dead, but you have to make sure. She's one of the stacked bodies behind you, if she isn't then she'll be in a doorway in a street off High Holborn. You have to get there—to High Holborn. It can't be far. This might be it—this stark desolate road. But it isn't.

You walk on and on, putting one foot before the other, holding your breath against the pain and fatigue. You call it walking, but it's not. It's a shuffling, shambling progression, animal-like, zombie-like—but it's a progression for all that. But the direction is wrong, brother. You're moving away from the fire, and High Holborn is in the direction of the fire. You'd better turn round and go back.

Funny how the thirst comes over you, quite suddenly. Strange to feel thirst at all. A few minutes ago it hadn't existed, and now it's here—a coarse sandpaper feeling in the throat and a tongue that feels dry and rough and enlarged. It's the smoke and the fire and the exposure. A glass of water would be welcome. A large glass of water and then a large glass of whisky. That's a laugh. There hasn't been any whisky in the world for a thousand years.

Look around for a while. Look at the bleak deserted shops with their smashed empty windows. Try to identify them. See anything you recognise, brother? That sign, about a hundred miles away, beyond the third block. The red and blue circular sign with the rectangular bar. An Underground station? Could be. Walk a little nearer, and nearer, until you can see the name. Still too far—the letters can't be resolved. Nearer still, and nearer. And there it is— the landmark you've been hunting for—the point of identification.

Kingsway.

A surge of energy in your body—a spasmodic beating of a tired heart. This is it, brother. Kingsway—the haven of safety. The I.B.I. in Consort Building, the familiar faces, the Waldorf, and the helicopters. The merciful helicopters. Turn back again. Cross the road. Down the right-hand side, down towards Aldwych. It's not far now. The next block. A few more yards. And here we are, brother. As easy as that. This is the Consort Building. It's in darkness, of course, but that's probably because the power has failed. No security guard on the door—that's careless, very careless. But go inside anyway, into the hollow darkness of the foyer, and down the shrouded stairs into the silent basement.

There's nobody here.

Colonel Brindle's office is empty. The Cypher office is empty. Your own office is empty. They've gone—all of them. They've left you behind. They've deserted you. And you were one of the survival group—but they've deserted you.

You're alone in a dying world.

★

When sanity returned, Wade found himself lying on the floor of his abandoned office in the Consort Building, crying uncontrollably. The tears stopped abruptly, and he became possessed by a vast impersonal defiance—a defiance of fate, of nature, and of God. He stumbled around in the darkness, wondering how he had ever found his way into the basement of the building, and returned to Kingsway.

It was night, but the darkness was pregnant with the ominous glare of the fire beyond the rooftops. Slowly he limped away from Aldwych towards the Underground station and High Holborn, and at the road junction by the inactive traffic lights he encountered a military patrol.

A flashlight swept over him and a harsh voice said: "Where d'you think you're going?"

"High Holborn," Wade said, appalled at the huskiness of his own voice. "I have to get to High Holborn."

"The entire area has been destroyed—and we're blowing up everything east of Tottenham Court Road in twenty minutes. Better get moving."

"Please," said Wade, "there's something I have to do..."

A boot moved swiftly in the darkness. Wade found himself rolling on his back gasping for breath.

"Get moving or be shot."

Wade picked himself up and staggered away from the probing beam of the inquisitive flashlight.

There was no bitterness or anger in him, only a cold impersonal acceptance of the facts of existence as they were in the here and now. He made his way towards New Oxford Street. London looked strange in the darkness—total darkness, without street lights, or traffic robots, or neon signs, or car headlamps. The roads were black caverns between the sheer sides of empty hollow buildings, leading from nowhere to nowhere.

This is the pay-off, he thought. Part of the final disintegration of civilised society. First the drought, and then the fire, and in time the fire would sweep the whole country and the whole world, because the natural antidote to fire no longer existed. Everything that would burn must inevitably burn sooner or later, and fire and disease would account for the mass of humanity.

The brutality was to be expected. It was part of the dehumanising process, the reduction of authority to more and more primitive levels. And in the end authority itself would disintegrate, and the military forces would themselves prey upon those they were assigned to protect, and then prey upon each other. And soon nothing would remain but isolated gangs and tribes, fighting for survival by the exercise of violence. The fire and the ice. Death and life.

In the polar zones life was going on in a normal if austere way, disciplined and principled. There were still ideals, and there was still chivalry, and humanity. Suddenly he felt immensely grateful that Janet was out of it all, and David too. They had been spared the final demoralisation, and all they would ever know of it would be second-hand reports and hearsay—not even eye-witness accounts, for the survivors would be those who had been sheltered from the harsh, unbelievable truth—who had not seen for themselves the rapid dissolution of a dying society.

The helicopter mission had been a mistake. There had been no necessity to observe the outside world and to witness the progress of the fire. It had been more than a mistake. It had been a tragedy. He had been responsible for the violent death of Susan, and had unwittingly cut himself off from his own kind. The evacuation of Consort Building had been rapidly and efficiently completed during his absence, and he could only conclude that the entire staff had been removed to the air base at Bletchley.

That then was his destination. It was the first stage on the return journey to his wife and child, and an essential step towards survival. Indeed, unless he could reach Bletchley swiftly and safely survival might well prove to be impossible.

He quickened the motion of his dragging feet, and soon found himself passing through a military cordon at the junction of Oxford Street and Tottenham Court Road.

"Step on it," they said. "We're blowing up the whole damn lot in seven minutes."

Wade pressed on in the darkness towards Oxford Circus, and now there were people, all moving west—thin haggard people, carrying cases and bundles, mostly men, but here and there an occasional woman ringed protectively by men. Hollow brittle people, like animated shells wrought in human shape. People with soulless eyes and desperate mouths. Hungry and thirsty people. And among them the weak, feverish people whose sunken dehydrated flesh hinted at cholera.

Wade had almost reached Argyll Street, home of the once famous Palladium, when the night sky exploded into garish yellow incandescence. The air pounded his ears with the tumult of detonated high explosive. Glancing back he saw London rearing up in an eruption of fire, and soon debris began to fall around him so that he was forced to seek shelter in a derelict shop doorway.

Step by step they were razing London to the ground, and step by step the great fire was advancing, leaping across the zones of shapeless destruction, pursuing the stubborn humans to the limits of the city. Inevitably they would blow up the West End as far as Park Lane, and then the high-explosive charges would be set in

Bayswater and Victoria and the Edgware Road, and so the final retreat would go on.

Near Bond Street he came upon a long queue of people and he took his place instinctively, not knowing what they were waiting for, but sensing that it must be worth waiting for. An hour and a half later he reached the head of the queue. On a long trestle table was a field kitchen, and uniformed figures were serving hot soup in tiny bowls not much larger than egg-cups. It was difficult to distinguish the uniform in the darkness, but he realised suddenly that it was the Salvation Army. An elderly woman in uniform handed him his tiny ration of soup with a compassion that he found almost incredible. He studied the details of her face in the gloom—a rough, kindly face, possessing a quality of calm peace that seemed almost radiant. And somehow, among the chaos and the violence, it didn't seem to make sense—not the kind of sense that he needed. But he acknowledged once more the ascendancy of the human spirit—just here and there—shining like a bright star in the blackest of nights.

He drank the mouthful of soup eagerly—it was watery, but welcome. No second helpings, but somehow he didn't feel resentful. He passed on, aware of a curious feeling of spiritual well-being, and presently found himself at the Marble Arch.

You need a programme, he told himself—a clear-cut programme for survival. Let's face it—you're suffering from shock, in bad shape, and you've lost blood—you may have cholera for all you know. The clothes you are wearing belonged to a cholera victim. You need water and food and sleep. How long can you expect to survive in such a condition? Two days—possibly three?

In that time, brother, you've got to make Bletchley. In less than that time. You have to get there before the last aircraft takes off for the Arctic. When will that be? It's anybody's guess. You have to be at Bletchley tomorrow, or sooner.

Okay—that's logical. But how to get there? You need a car or a truck. No such things—except for a few military vehicles. So you have to steal a military truck. For that you need weapons. A knife, or a cosh, or a gun. And to use a weapon you need strength, and that means you must sleep.

So where can a guy sleep in comfort and safety? Break into a house, maybe—but the occupants would be hostile and as desperate as yourself. You need to have a friend—someone you can rely on, like Shirley Sye in the old days.

He wondered about Shirley. Maybe she was dead, or maybe she had moved away, or maybe she was still making the best of life, if that's what you called it, in her shabby apartment in Lawrence Avenue. At all events he was at the bottom end of the Edgware Road, and Maida Vale was not too far away. He could walk it, slowly, in about half an hour.

I'll do that, he said aloud.

Funny thing really—to think that he had once walked out on Shirley, an eternity ago, it seemed, and now he was going back to her. That was a great joke. Even Shirley would have to laugh at that one.

The journey took longer than he thought, and it was fully an hour before he reached number seventeen Lawrence Avenue.

The front door was open, and the staircase had been stripped of carpet. He made his way upwards wearily, but with caution. The apartment was dark and silent, and there was a smell that he found repulsive.

On the landing he stopped and said: "Shirley!"

Silence mocked him.

He moved forward, arms outstretched, until he touched the cold smooth surface of a wall. He ran his hand along it until he reached a door, and felt for the knob. He went in.

The darkness was absolute, and in this room the abhorrent smell was stronger. It was the smell of staleness and decay—perhaps even the smell of death. He hesitated uncertainly.

"Shirley," he said quietly.

He moved forward again, very slowly, until his legs touched something. Feeling with his hands he identified a bed. Shirley's bedroom. That was lucky, and it might have been the answer to a prayer. All he needed was a bed and the chance to sleep for a few hours, until daylight.

With a sigh he sat on the edge of the bed, then allowed his body to fall slowly backwards. The coverings were rumpled, and the sheet was chill and stiff; as his weight came upon it the material crackled and the smell of decay became more pungent. But he was in no mood to care. Exhausted to the point of coma he allowed the tension of his body to relax, and fell immediately into a deep, dreamless sleep.

XII

WADE WAS AWAKENED BY LOUD EXPLOSIONS THAT SEEMED to shake the entire house. He was alert in an instant, groping in the confusion of his mind for memory and detail, and in a moment it all came back to him, and he groaned in utter weariness of spirit. Harsh sunlight was streaming through the curtainless window, glaring on faded patterned wallpaper, and illuminating the bed.

He got up and stared at the incredible condition of the sheet on which he had lain, not understanding the opaque discoloration that lay on it like brittle enamel—and then, abruptly, he realised that the entire bed was caked with the black-brown of dried blood. Perhaps Shirley's blood? He had no way of finding out.

But the revulsion within him was a dispirited thing. He pushed the transient ghostly image of Shirley out of his mind and went out of the bedroom, walking lamely, his body stiff and painful. He went into the living room, now bare and stripped of furniture, and found himself face to face with a frail little man whose chin sprouted a wispy white beard. The little man was grinning toothlessly and holding a carving knife in bony fleshless fingers.

"Been waitin' for you," said the man in a high, cracked voice. "You got no right to be here. This is my place."

"Since when?" Wade asked, weighing up his opponent.

"Since two weeks. You got no right to be here."

"The woman who used to live here—did you kill her?"

"I never killed anyone. She was dead when I came here. Throat cut clean as a whistle. Job I had getting rid of the body—you wouldn't believe…"

"She was a friend of mine."

The little man shifted uneasily on his feet. "Well just you get out of here, anyway. I don't want no trouble. Things is bad enough."

Wade reached out and took the knife from the other with a minimum of effort. He inspected it thoughtfully, then slipped it inside his shirt.

"You got no right to do that. You got no right to be here…"

"No more have you," Wade said harshly, advancing a pace.

The little man backed away nervously. "I don't want no trouble. She was dead when I came here. Found the place open and empty. Just her—lying dead. I thought I'd live up here for a bit. Got me some food and water…"

"Where?"

The little man cackled, and cunning flickered in his eyes for an instant. "That's a secret. I've known men get themselves murdered for a can of water. But while it's a secret I can bargain with you. I ain't got long to go, anyway. I'm seventy-six. Not long to go. Why should I care?"

"I'm not a killer," said Wade. "Not yet, anyway. I know how to escape from all this. How to get to the Arctic. That's where I'm going, as soon as I've finished here."

"You don't," said the little man incredulously.

Wade grinned faintly. "But I do. All I have to do is get to a certain place, about forty miles from here. There are aeroplanes waiting."

"Forty miles is a long way, mister. You'll never make it."

"I will. I'm going to steal a military truck. And I'm going to steal guns. I'll make it."

The little man began to tremble with excitement. He came close to Wade and took his hand. "I do believe you mean it. I do believe so. Take me with you, mister. That's all I ask. Take me with you."

Wade framed his thoughts with dispassionate deliberation. "I might even do that. But first I need water and food."

"I've *got* water and food," the old man said eagerly. "Had a son who did some Black Market deals. Got hisself shot by the troops. Left me a crate of water cans and Heinz beans. You can share them. Only take me with you."

"Where are they?" Wade asked.

The little man moved towards the door, and Wade followed him into the bedroom, beyond the bed, to a corner of the room near the window. There the old man bent down and lifted a corner of the worn lino, then removed a section of floorboard. Wade stooped and peered into the cavity.

There were about a dozen cans in the shadows under the floorboards, half of them green and labelled *Water*, and the others bearing a printed label depicting beans in tomato sauce. A banquet indeed, thought Wade, in these days of universal famine. He stood up and eyed the old man speculatively.

"I've played ball with you," said the other. "You'll take me with you now, won't you?"

I can't kill him, Wade thought. Not in cold blood when there's no threat. If he were like the others, there would be no problem—in a world of mad dogs one can be a mad dog too, and to hell with conscience. While there are still a few ordinary people about who haven't lost their humanity, then they have to be treated with humanity—or does that make sense? If I don't kill him, then someone else will. He's going to die anyway, when his little stockpile of food and water runs out, and the chances are he'll be robbed of it before then...

"You promised," insisted the old man, catching Wade's arm eagerly. "I've done my bit—now you'll have to take me with you."

Wade shook off the frail fingers with an impatient gesture. "I didn't promise anything," he pointed out. "Two of us would never make it. I may not even be able to make it on my own."

For an instant the old man's lips trembled, so that Wade thought he was about to cry, and then he went berserk. He leaped at Wade with incredible agility, shaking him and clawing at him with his skeletal fingers. "You *promised!*" he shrieked. "You *promised!*"

The unexpected impetus of the attack nearly floored Wade, but he grasped the window ledge and maintained his balance. A moment later he pushed the old man away, clenched his fist, hesitated for an instant, then knocked him down. The slight body crashed to the floor, twitched for a while, then became still. Wade stroked his knuckles thoughtfully.

You'll have to get used to it, brother, he told himself. This is the way it's going to be, all along the line. If you let sentiment get a hold, then you're finished. You have to do business with the devil for the right to live.

He bent down and inspected the old man, satisfying himself that he was still alive, then he set about the cans with the carving knife, working quickly and with an uneasy sense of guilt and dejection. He ate two cans of beans and gulped down two pints of water. Then, as a precaution, he stuffed a can of water into the pocket of his trousers. Regretfully he surveyed the remaining cans—four of beans and three of water. Well, at least the old man would still have his feast.

He replaced the cans under the floorboards, then, noticing that the old man was stirring, quietly left the apartment and made his way down to the street.

Stealing a vehicle had not been so difficult after all, Wade reflected as he drove at a steady fifty miles per hour along the road to Bletchley. The vehicle was a small 15-cwt. Bedford truck, and it had been parked outside a garrison headquarters near Kilburn, in charge of a sergeant driver and guarded by a corporal armed with a tommy-gun who paced the pavement and forced the few pedestrians and stragglers to make a detour.

Wade, ignoring the corporal's truculent gesture, had approached him cautiously, making as if he wished to talk to him, and then he stumbled and fell, deliberately, knocking the corporal's feet from under him. Almost before the sergeant in the truck had realised what was happening, Wade was in possession of the tommy-gun. The corporal, cursing luridly, grappled at his legs, and as Wade kicked himself free, the sergeant produced a revolver and fired twice, but his aim was uncertain. Wade didn't stop to argue, but shot the sergeant there and then, and, opening the door of the cab, pulled his body out and left it on the pavement.

Within seconds he was driving furiously up Edgware Road, with the tommy-gun resting on the empty passenger seat beside him. The burst of machine-gun fire that came from behind was already too distant to matter.

At Canon's Park he shot his way through a road block, and again at Watford, relying on speed, surprise and ruthlessness to get him through. And good luck, of course. Despite the odds he was still free and still alive, and his fatigue was slowly giving way to a sense of exultance. Another half an hour, he told himself, and I'll be back with my own kind—back with the survival group.

Driving from Leighton Buzzard towards Bletchley on the final lap he realised suddenly that he had no real idea where the aerodrome was located. He stopped the truck and surveyed the panorama of the bleak, lifeless countryside that shivered and wavered in the sunglare, seeking a landmark, but there was nothing, only the brown dehydrated shells of trees and deserted farm buildings. He drove on and presently came upon a forest of steel pylons and masts spread over a large field. This, he assumed, was where the I.B.I. aerials had been installed, the huge rhombic aerials beamed at I.B.I. communication points in other continents. Somewhere close at hand would be the now inoperative I.B.I. transmitting and receiving station, and, logically, perhaps, the aerodrome.

While he was ruminating in this way he became aware of the sound of gunfire. Again he stopped the truck and listened carefully to the remote staccato crackling, and behind it was another sound, subdued and swamped by the noise of the truck engine. He switched off the ignition, and immediately recognised the characteristic whine of a jet engine running up. Alarm clutched momentarily at his heart. He made a rough computation of the direction from which the noise was coming, then got back in the truck and drove off.

He came upon the aerodrome suddenly. It emerged upon him in its wide functional flatness as he rounded a bend in the road. It was not so much an aerodrome as an airstrip, probably a reconditioned derelict from the last war, and the new extended runway of steel planking gleamed blue-grey in the sunlight. In the foreground was a small group of control buildings, and at the remote end of the runway, perhaps a quarter of a mile distant, or more, stood a single white jet airliner.

Wade stopped the truck and made a more detailed survey of the scene. The gunfire seemed to be coming from a black tangle of dead hedging about a hundred yards from the control tower, and as he walked nearer and his angle of view changed, he observed a large group of khaki-clad men behind the hedging. There was a machine gun, and there were rifles and carbines, and a heavy wooden box that might have contained hand grenades.

They were shooting towards the control tower, and now he could see their target. Parked in front of the tower on the concrete strip at the near end of the runway was a small single-decker bus, painted olive-green, with a Royal Air Force roundel on the side. The windows of the bus had been smashed, and the sides were heavily punctured with bullet holes. Behind the bus he saw another group of people—about twenty or twenty-five men and women in civilian clothes, with a sprinkling of khaki-clad figures who looked like officers.

The situation began to crystallise in Wade's mind. He glanced from the bus to the jetliner and then to the hedging with the machine-gun nest. It looked as if the troops guarding the airstrip had finally rebelled against the arbitrary nature of the survival evacuation programme. They had seized a commanding position between the control tower and the aircraft and obviously had no intention of allowing the prospective passengers hiding behind the wrecked bus to make their escape. Whether their plans were any more advanced than that, Wade was unable to guess, but he imagined the mutiny had been spontaneous rather than premeditated.

The men and women behind the bus were probably the last remnants of the I.B.I. team awaiting evacuation to the

Arctic—perhaps even his own colleagues from Kingsway. But the balance of power was against them. True, they had a few revolvers, and were returning the insurgent fire at erratic intervals, but the troops had the supreme advantage of automatic weapons.

Wade debated the problem for a long time, trying to determine where his allegiance lay. He was in a good position to make a suicidal rear attack on the mutineers, but there was no hope of gaining control of the situation, and he didn't feel like suicide. He looked across the length of the runway to the distant jetliner, and now he could see that the fuselage door was open and minute figures were standing there, staring out of the cabin.

I've got to be impersonal about the whole damn business, Wade told himself. I've got to be a realist. I can't differentiate between the good and the bad, and in the long run it doesn't matter. In a situation like this the devil takes the hindmost. They all want to survive, every goddam human being on the planet, and right now we're back where evolution left off—before the dawn of civilisation. There's no entitlement to life—it has to be preserved by tooth and claw—more than that, by cunning.

He paused reflectively. There was still time to think and observe and make a decision, but the act of deciding required a number of basic motivating factors—things such as loyalty, morality, ethics—abstract things that seemed to have no proper place in this disintegrating society. What was it Shirley Sye had said so many thousands of years ago in the days when she had lived and breathed? *In a crisis people revert to some fundamental level... behaviour is dominated by a survival drive.* That was about the truth of the matter. Pity Shirley hadn't profited by her wisdom. *The general adaptation syndrome.* Hats off to Shirley. So what does the syndrome say? Survive first and ask questions afterwards? That was axiomatic—you couldn't ask questions if you failed to survive.

I've done things I never thought possible, he thought, in a kind of spiritual desperation. I've killed men—but then, they would have killed me. I've come to accept violence and brutality, and I've desensitised myself to things that would have shocked me into insanity a few months ago. I've been confronted with sudden death—and yet there was no impact, or rather, the impact was swamped by the overall impact of the death of the human species—the physical, moral and spiritual death. Hell, I never did react much, but now I react less and less with every passing minute.

Let's add up the score, brother. The world survives so long as you survive. At the moment of death the world comes to an end for you, and it has no further reality in the darkness of that other strange dimension. Maybe you've tried, in your own fashion, to do the decent thing among the gross indecencies of the day, but there's only one decent thing left to do, and that's to get back to Janet and young David, to restore the solid bond of the family and protect their future. All the mistakes and heartaches of the past—they don't matter any more. The future can be moulded…

The people in front of you now, shooting at each other in a final frantic gamble for the last plane out, are already empty shadows. They're your enemies—every one of them. They're studying their own interests, and they're all conforming to the survival behaviour pattern. You've got to play them at their own game and win, brother. There's a long journey ahead, and you're on your own—alone and unaided.

Abruptly Wade made up his mind. He returned to the truck and took out the tommy-gun, then walked lamely back towards the aerodrome.

Near to the hedging, still unobserved, he crawled under the wire of the perimeter fence, and continued crawling towards the khaki-clad group. He managed to get within twenty yards of them before he was spotted, and in a fraction of a second half a dozen weapons were pointing at him.

"No," he shouted, "I'm a friend. I'm on your side."

One of them came towards him, a burly red-faced corporal swinging a Sten gun. Revolvers crackled from the direction of the control tower, and the corporal threw himself on the ground, pointing the Sten at Wade.

"We don't want no passengers," he growled.

"Look," Wade said urgently. "I can help. Even if you take that plane you'll never be able to fly it. The crew will fight it out to the end and they'll sabotage it rather than give it up."

"Not if we're quick enough."

"You never could be. And if you forced the issue the plane could always take off in a hurry and abandon the lot of you—the passengers too. Why do you suppose the jets are running up?"

"Then what do you suggest?"

"I'm a qualified pilot. I can fly the plane."

"We still have to take it."

"We have to be subtle. I have a plan which may work."

The corporal eyed him speculatively for several seconds. "We could use a plan, if you're on the level, and you'd better be on the level for your own sake. Come on."

He led the way back to the group, and Wade followed, keeping close to the ground and never relaxing his grip on the tommy-gun.

There were about forty-five of them all together, mainly young men in battledress—dirty unshaven young men perspiring in the intense heat of the unshielded sun. But they were probably less dirty and unshaven than he was himself, Wade reflected. They were a mob, but not an undisciplined mob, and he was not slow to realise that they needed strong, decisive leadership. He took the initiative immediately.

"Who's in charge?" he demanded.

"I am," said the corporal. "Name of Bates. Corporal Fred Bates."

Wade nodded. "All right, Fred. I'm Philip Wade—one time pilot, ex-journalist, and until recently a government official."

"He ain't one of us, Fred," said a different voice.

"Shut up," Fred ordered. "Listen to what Mr. Wade's got to say. He may have ideas. None of us here ain't."

"All right," Wade said, reclining uncomfortably on one arm. "First you've got to put me in the picture. Who's in the plane right now?"

"The crew—four of them—and about six others—the brass hats."

"How did all this start?"

"Well, it really started when food and water supplies were cut off—about three days ago. We heard about the fire in London, and the plague. Then the airlift was doubled. Helicopters started bringing hundreds of civvies in, and jets took them away day and night. And then, last night, the civvies stopped arriving and the planes stopped coming. This here jet landed about two hours ago and got ready for take-off right away. So we begins to wonder what's going on. We're all thirsty and hungry and a bit bloody-minded."

Wade remembered the can of water in his pocket, but decided to keep it to himself. The future was still very uncertain.

"So we got hold of one of the civvies and beat him up a bit, just to get the truth out of him. He said this was the last plane out of Bletchley—perhaps out of England. There was nothing anyone could do any more. The plague and fire were uncontrollable."

"All that plus thirst and hunger," Wade added.

"He said most of the people in this country would be dead within ten days."

"Probably right."

"So me and the boys had what you might call a conference. We didn't see as how we should be left behind. We decided to take over the plane, but we weren't quite quick enough. We've got most of the civvies and brass hats trapped behind the bus that was to take them over to the plane, but half a dozen went over in a staff car."

Wade stared steadily at the corporal, considering his words. "You realise you're in a spot. If you attempt to rush the plane it will take off. If you wipe out the civvies by the control tower it will still take off. If you play the waiting game you may find reinforcements coming up, or even bombers assigned to eliminate you. They're probably in radio contact with Air Force units right now—assuming any kind of military discipline exists anywhere in the country. At all events you can't afford to take that chance, and you can't afford to waste time."

"So what do we do?"

Wade stroked his chin thoughtfully. There were almost fifty soldiers in the group and the jet plane was probably already booked for its full complement of about thirty. They couldn't all survive, whatever happened, and that in itself threatened an ugly situation. But a plan was beginning to shape itself in his mind.

"Who's in charge of the civvies?" he asked.

"A civvy with a military handle. A Colonel Brindle."

Wade smiled grimly. "Interesting."

"He's in the plane."

"Fine. Now listen, Fred—Brindle is, or was, a colleague of mine. I know him pretty well. This is where we have to talk with the enemy."

"Talk?"

"A flag of truce."

The corporal spat on the ground. "The white flag counts for nothing. They'd shoot you down just the same—same as we would."

"Agreed. There is no place for honour. Brindle would shoot you just as you would shoot him. But he knows me. We're friends. He'd let me talk to him under the white flag."

"Not by yourself, you don't," said the corporal sceptically. "We are all in this together. What's to stop you using the white flag to get on the plane?"

"You can come with me, and one other man."

"It's too risky. They'd shoot us down long before they could recognise you, and long before we could get near the plane."

"We don't go to the plane," said Wade. "We go to the control tower. We're in a position to negotiate with the civvies—after all, we could wipe them out in one single assault."

"And lose the plane."

"Of course—but that doesn't make *them* feel any better. They're in the same boat as you or me, hoping against hope for the chance to survive. They can't get to the plane any more than we can, so they'll be ready to negotiate."

"Negotiate *what*?" growled one of the soldiers in the intently listening throng.

"Negotiate an interview with Colonel Brindle under a flag of truce. We get them to call the plane on radiotelephone from the control tower. They send a message that Philip Wade wants to talk to the Colonel. Then three of us go over—unarmed."

"Are you crazy?"

"Unarmed to all appearances. We can carry revolvers concealed in our clothing. Meanwhile, one of your men has to work his way unseen to the offside of the plane, as close as he can. He has to be a marksman, and he will need a good rifle."

"That'll be Geordie," said the Corporal. "He can hit a mosquito at a hundred yards blindfold. And he's got a rifle with telescopic sights."

"I was a sniper in the last war," said the chunky, red-faced man called Geordie.

"Fine," Wade commented. "Well, Geordie takes up a position where he can see the pilot. That should be easy enough. The pilot will be at the controls, ready for a quick take-off if necessary. Three of us will go over to the plane to talk with Colonel Brindle. I will make the first move—I'll shoot Brindle." He turned to the sniper. "Geordie—as soon as you hear the shot, you pick off the pilot. Then we all of us deal with whoever is left in the plane, whether they put up a fight or not. As soon as the shooting starts the rest of you lob a couple of hand grenades behind the bus to create confusion, then come over to the plane as quickly as possible."

"Sounds a good scheme," Geordie murmured with satisfaction.

The corporal nodded in silent approval.

Sure it's a good scheme, Wade thought. A spontaneous scheme, creating itself out of mental vacuum, word by word. A cold, bloody, brutal scheme, detailed in a voice that I didn't even recognise as my own. A scheme to fit the circumstances. What's happened to me? Was I always like this, or am I changing through a vicious process of conditioning, like one of Pavlov's dogs? A mental pause. I'll think about it later, when it's all over. I'll have the rest of my life to hate myself in, but first I have to secure that life. Survival is top priority.

He said: "It will be a good scheme if everything goes according to plan. No mistakes, and that applies particularly to you, Geordie. The pilot *must* be killed first time. He's the key man. Without him they can't take off."

Geordie smiled thinly and patted his rifle.

"Colonel Brindle has to die, too," Wade continued dispassionately. "He's the leader, and any group deprived of its leader is confused for a time. It's up to us to take advantage of that confusion."

"Don't worry," said the corporal.

Wade held out a hand that trembled slightly. "I want a revolver, and I want one of you to make a white flag of truce."

Somebody pushed a compact automatic pistol into his hand. He inspected it without reaction, aware of a cold ghostly hand gripping his heart, then slipped it into his pocket.

If only they knew, he told himself—if only they knew what was really here in my mind... But they wouldn't believe. They wouldn't understand the cold single-mindedness of a desperate man. I don't even understand it myself. But it has to be done, brother. It has to be done—starting here and now.

"Halt," commanded Colonel Brindle.

Wade halted, as did the corporal and the other soldier behind him. Brindle was some twenty feet away, and he had walked forward some twenty-five yards from the plane. That was awkward enough, Wade thought, but even worse was the sub-machine gun in the hands of the man sitting in the open doorway of the fuselage cabin. It wasn't going to be so easy, after all.

"I can see that you are Philip Wade after all," Brindle said. "You don't look much like him."

"I've been living rough," said Wade.

"You crossed the fence, Wade. We had to strike you off the list. And Miss Vance."

"Miss Vance is dead," said Wade, stepping forward.

"Stay where you are," Brindle ordered. "I'll speak plainly. I've nothing to say to you, Wade, and nothing to discuss. Neither you nor the pack you have joined will set foot in this aircraft. I strongly advise you, in the name of humanity, to let the other passengers join us, but it doesn't matter if you don't."

"I don't hear much humanity in what you have to say," Wade countered, wondering whether Geordie was in position and waiting. "These men have as much right to survival as your passengers. We thought you might agree to a deal."

"What kind of deal?"

"Your women passengers, and as many of our men as you can get aboard."

"No," Brindle said firmly. "It is more important to keep your kind out than to let our kind in. Once you have been touched by violence you lose something for ever. We don't want people with that kind of twist in their minds. We'd rather close the door on all of you here, good and bad alike, than risk contamination. We have a new world to build, Wade, and we want to make it a good clean world."

"You're doing a mighty lot of judging, Colonel," Wade said sourly. "What makes you think *you're* a suitable citizen for a brave new world? What human qualities have you ever shown in this crisis?"

"I obeyed orders, Wade, and my final duty is to differentiate between those entitled to survive... and the rest."

"By what divine right do you take it upon yourself to determine the matter of life and death?"

Brindle pointed to the armed man in the cabin door of the aircraft. "My divine right is there. It's the only kind of right that has any influence now." A pause, then: "I'm sorry it has to end this way, Wade. We're much of a kind, you and I. If you were in my position you'd do exactly the same."

"And if you were me...?" Wade enquired.

Brindle eyed him narrowly, then shook his head. "You used to have a good heart—good enough, at any rate. But right now I don't know you."

Wade said nothing. Time was running out.

"Call off your men and let the passengers join the aircraft," Brindle snapped. "It's the last decent action left to you. I'll give you thirty minutes—then we take off anyway."

Wade grinned faintly and with irony. "The heroic Colonel Brindle! You were dead right. We're much of a kind, but maybe I've got a bit more of it than you. Is that your last word?"

Brindle nodded.

It had to be now—there could be no further compromise. Wade turned reluctantly, exchanged tense glances with the corporal, made as if to walk away from the jetliner, then quickly and desperately drew the pistol from his pocket, flung himself to the ground, and fired. Brindle clawed at his chest, and there was stark understanding in his eyes. Wade fired again. The Colonel toppled backwards and writhed on the ground.

"Brindle, I'm sorry, but it had to be," Wade murmured. The sub-machine gun chattered angrily and the ground around him was flaked and churned by whining bullets.

And then the corporal and his comrade were firing their revolvers, and the sub-machine gun had stopped, and the man in the aircraft was toppling forward.

Wade had reached his worst moment. "Get in there," he said, from his position on the ground. "Finish them all off. I'll be right behind you."

The two men went ahead, and at the same moment Geordie appeared round the tail of the plane, grinning cheerfully. He made a thumbs-up sign at Wade, and joined the others. Wade picked himself up with deliberate slowness, dragging his feet as he walked towards the aircraft. The air was filled with the sound of shooting and wild cries and groans.

Remotely from behind came the thunder of more powerful explosions. He did not look back. The plan was proceeding to schedule. After the hand grenades the pack would be converging on the jetliner as quickly as their legs could carry them. He had about half a minute to do what he had to do.

He reached the door of the aircraft and looked inside. The three men were mopping up, and their backs were turned to him. He did not hesitate. Three times he fired, then a fourth time to make sure. He climbed inside the plane and slammed the door.

The corporal was still alive, and his eyes were full of incredulous malevolence. He moved his lips to speak, but only blood issued forth. Wade shot him between the eyes; he couldn't afford to take chances.

The pilot was sprawled across the controls in the cockpit. Wearily Wade heaved his body out of the way, noting academically the precision with which Geordie had placed the bullet into his victim's brow. He took his seat and ran his hands over the controls. Through the window he could see the advancing horde—close, too close—not more than fifty yards away.

Calmly, without feeling, he took possession of the aircraft, moving forward at gathering speed, forcing power into the jets, screaming towards the control tower and the carnage behind the shattered bus. Steadily he pulled back on the control column. The jetliner lifted perceptibly, and the dark sterile ground fell slowly away.

At ten thousand feet he switched in the automatic pilot and returned to the passenger cabin. There wasn't much energy left in him, he realised that, but one more job had to be done. He jettisoned the cabin door, then, one by one, dragged the bodies strewn over the floor to the opening and pushed them out. Twenty minutes later he returned to the pilot's seat. Cursorily he inspected the instruments. The compass was set at due north and the automatic pilot held the plane in its inflexible grip.

He sighed deeply and rubbed his forehead. A great tenseness drained suddenly from him. It's over, he told himself. The nightmare is over. It was all a dream, an irrational dream, and soon I shall wake up and be with Janet and David, and we'll pick up life where we left off. An imperfect life, perhaps. Life is never perfect for any of us.

He pondered the nightmare for a while. Remorse darkened his mind. I touched rock bottom, he told himself. But I wasn't myself. I was in the grip of the syndrome—Shirley's syndrome. Brindle was just part of the equation—a simultaneous equation in life and death. He knew it, just as I knew it.

The weariness dissolved fractionally, giving way to sullen anger. To hell with Brindle. He was no better than any of us. Worse than most, if you took the moral viewpoint. He was one of the survival group leaders, and he took it upon himself to allocate the right to live and die. He had the Piercey mentality—dispassionate, egocentric, unconcerned. For an instant Wade recalled the Salvation Army woman at the soup kitchen in Oxford Street on the previous night, and the image of her calm, compassionate features flitted briefly through his mind, and he compared her with the impersonal arrogance of Colonel Brindle. *It is more important to keep your kind out than to let our kind in*—that was what Brindle had said, and it typified the singular autocracy of his outlook. Wade aligned himself with the Salvation Army woman, with the mass of doomed humanity as a whole. It's our kind that Brindle hated, the ordinary people, the people who had to die so that he might live. Well, things had worked out differently.

The trend of his thinking shifted. There was a girl in my dream called Susan, he recalled. Funny thing, I can't even remember her face any more. But I avenged her. And a woman called Shirley. I avenged her too. And I've avenged myself, for what it's worth.

He closed his eyes, soothed by the vibration of the jets. The plane screamed northwards through the grey sky. I'm leaving the world behind, he thought, and in ten days it will be all over. And we, the ordinary people, will be a dead species, and the calculating soulless ones will inherit the earth. We—the betrayed!

But there was something wrong in the concept, and he pondered it drowsily. I'm deceiving myself, he admitted. I'm not really one of the ordinary people, nor am I really one of the survival group any more. He grimaced and laughed shortly. That was Philip Wade all over—neither one thing nor the other. The jack of all trades, master of none. Would-be husband, journalist, lover, alcoholic, government official, rebel, tough guy and killer. Latter-day prophet. *Is The Tide Going Out For Ever?* The man with the flexible conscience. The opportunist who never lacked opportunity. The noble and responsible character who took to ruthless violence like a duck to water.

Brindle was right. Once you've been touched by violence you lose something for ever. But for ever is an overstatement. You can only lose something for a lifetime, and you can tolerate a loss for a lifetime.

He opened his eyes for a moment to glance outwards towards the drab brown wilderness that was England. In the course of time, he thought, Davey will return with others to rehabilitate this barren tormented land, but it won't be in my time. There are oceans to fill, and fields to plant and cultivate, and cities to build. And the dead to bury.

Presently he fell asleep, and the jetliner flew north at a level altitude of ten thousand feet.

They shot him down with radar-controlled anti-aircraft guns just south of the Arctic Circle.

Years later, on his fourteenth birthday, young David said to his mother: "If I'd been Dad I'd have got back. I'd have fought everyone and I'd have stolen an aeroplane, but I'd have got back."

Janet smiled and shook her head sadly. "Your father wasn't like that, Davey. There was a lot of good in him. I think, perhaps, when it came to the point, and the end was near, he chose to stay behind."

"But why?"

"To help people. To try to make things easier. It was the kind of thing he would be likely to do."

"Didn't he *want* to come back to us?"

The Arctic wind howled across the corrugated roof of the prefabricated hut, but the room glowed with the warmth of atomic heating. Janet put her arm on the boy's shoulders.

"Of course he wanted to come back, Davey. But there are times when a man has to do what he thinks is right. He has to be strong—to give his life, if that's the way it has to be. Your daddy was like that."

The boy nodded, satisfied. "Dad sure must have been a fine man."

"Yes, a fine man," she echoed. She continued to smile, until her lips began to ache with the effort.

ALSO AVAILABLE BY CHARLES ERIC MAINE

BRITISH LIBRARY

THE DARKEST OF NIGHTS

CHARLES ERIC MAINE

SCIENCE FICTION CLASSICS